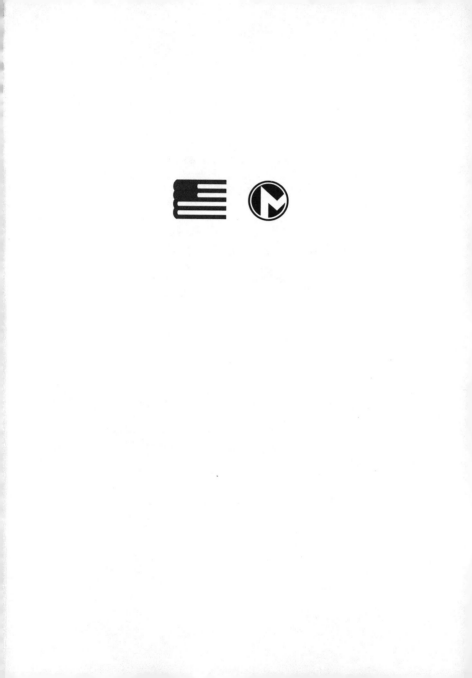

ALSO BY GLENN BECK

*It IS About Islam: Exposing the Truth About
ISIS, Al Qaeda, and the Caliphate*

*Dreamers and Deceivers: True Stories of
the Heroes and Villains Who Made America*

*Miracles and Massacres: True and Untold
Stories of the Making of America*

The Eye of Moloch

Control: Exposing the Truth About Guns

Agenda 21

Cowards: What Politicians, Radicals, and the Media Refuse to Say

*Being George Washington: The Indispensable Man,
as You've Never Seen Him*

Snow Angel

*The Original Argument: The Federalists' Case for
the Constitution, Adapted for the 21st Century*

GLENN BECK

The Immortal Nicholas

THRESHOLD EDITIONS :: MERCURY RADIO ARTS

New York   London   Toronto   Sydney   New Delhi

Threshold Editions/Mercury Radio Arts
An Imprint of Simon & Schuster, Inc.
1230 Avenue of the Americas
New York, NY 10020

First Threshold Editions/Mercury Radio Arts hardcover edition October 2015

THRESHOLD EDITIONS and colophon are trademarks of
Simon & Schuster, Inc.

GLENN BECK is a trademark of Mercury Radio Arts, Inc.

For information about special discounts for bulk purchases, please contact Simon & Schuster Special Sales at 1-866-506-1949 or business@simonandschuster.com.

The Simon & Schuster Speakers Bureau can bring authors to your live event. For more information or to book an event, contact the Simon & Schuster Speakers Bureau at 866-248-3049 or visit our website at www.simonspeakers.com.

Interior design by Jessica Shatan Heslin/Studio Shatan, Inc.

Manufactured in the United States of America

10 9 8 7 6 5 4 3 2 1

Library of Congress Cataloging-in-Publication Data is available.

ISBN 978-1-4767-9884-4
ISBN 978-1-4767-9890-5 (ebook)

To the children of the world, no matter their age,
who still believe in the real meaning of Christmas

PART I

Chapter 1

Sometimes death is a simple thing. A slip of the foot, a shift in the wind, a fall.

Agios had faced death often in his thirty-three years. He had been an adventurer, a hunter, and—to tell the truth—something of a rogue. He had always expected to die by violence, his blood spilled and his body racked with agony.

After he married the gentle foreigner named Weala, though, he had begun to consider his ways of life and death. For her sake he hoped that when his time came he would die well, as a man, not crying like a child or pleading for mercy. When their son Philos was born, Agios wanted even more to be strong for him.

For years the boy had been begging to go with his father to the savagely dangerous land of bare sun-struck stone and rocky crags. Now they stood together, a muscular, broad-shouldered man with flowing midnight-black hair and long black beard, and beside him a thin-limbed lad of only ten. The previous winter Weala had died in premature childbirth, along with Philos's stillborn younger brother. The loss of his mother had left the boy pale and unsmiling and had left Agios feeling that his heart had turned to lead.

And so Philos's coming with him on this trip was not a gift, but a necessity, for Agios had no one to watch over the boy. It had hurt, though, that the first faint smile that Agios had seen on his son's face in months had flickered there for a moment when Agios said, "Let's go gather frankincense."

Now they stood at the top of the cliffs where the trees grew, looking down the sheer rock face. Agios had already taken the resin from the first small grove of trees they had come to, and now they had reached the true orchard of wealth. "And you must pay close attention," Agios told Philos, and the boy nodded solemnly. "You must take care. The resin is more valuable than gold because it is so hard to find and collect. We will sell it to traders on their way to Egypt, Greece, Rome, or even India. What we collect in one day lets us live for a whole year."

Philos nodded impatiently. "I know, Father."

"You've seen the dangers when you've watched me gather the resin. Remember how careful I've been and do the same things. You understand?"

"Yes, Father."

Philos looked eager for the perilous work, and Agios well understood the intoxication of it. The resin offered rich reward at high risk. Of course his son was captivated. He had counted the days until he could follow in his father's steps.

The libanos trees, hunched and gnarled, clung to the cliff like weary climbers. At the pitch of noon, no wind stirred their branches. Many months earlier Agios had climbed down to make careful incisions in the flaking bark so that the golden tears would flow and dry. Anyone else who discovered this remote ravine with its precious trees might try to investigate, but they would soon hear the hiss of snakes twining among the branches—or feel the fatal sting of their fangs. Agios had deliberately established this colony of adders, now guards of the precarious grove.

Knowing the serpents were there made all the difference. Together, father and son threw rocks at the snakes, forcing them to lower branches, to trees farther from the edge where Agios had marked Philos's first tree. Because of Weala's death, Agios had waited longer than usual to harvest, and the resin was nearly dry in the slash marks, golden and fragrant. That made the frankincense even more valuable.

Agios knelt beside his son and looped a coil of rope around the boy's waist. "When you gather the flakes, remember they're worth more than everything we own," he said. "It's a great responsibility."

"Yes, Father."

"Be careful," Agios said one last time. He tossed a few more rocks to make sure the snakes had retreated, then tugged the rope to test it and put his big hand on his son's neck. He bent the scruffy head and inhaled the warm, woody scent of Philos's hair.

Before they had set out, Agios had scattered the dust of his last harvest of frankincense over the coals in their cabin. Philos now carried the lingering aroma of it, like pine and lemon and earth. To Agios, frankincense smelled exactly like his son.

Philos drew back grinning, his excitement palpable. He

edged toward the drop, his eagerness saying that this was not the time for affection, but for *action*.

Agios looped the free end of the rope around his own waist and took in the slack. Philos had grown up in the high mountains and he did not falter when he lowered himself over the rocky edge, rope tight, knees bent, feet braced on stone. A misstep sent a shower of stones and gravel tumbling down the escarpment, but Philos adjusted himself and made it safely to the tree.

Agios found his son's weight absurdly easy to bear, but just in case, he had doubled the rope around his own waist. Philos's life depended on its not slipping. He leaned back and watched his boy find and peel off the bubbled resin, the small sun-browned hands tucking each lump carefully away in a leather pouch at his waist before moving on to the next. Pride tightened Agios's throat, pride and the sort of love that reminded him that everything else he had loved in life now lived only in the boy.

Agios knew Philos was taking too long, but this was his first time. He did not urge the boy to hurry, because haste meant mistakes. He saw him brace his feet and reach deep into the heart of the gnarled branches.

Then Philos screamed and jerked.

He flung his arm wide. A snake clung to it for a half-heartbeat, then fell loose, tumbling, writhing.

Philos's agonized face arched back, and he shouted, "Father!"

Though it had happened in less than a second, Agios was already hauling on the rope, his hands strong and sure while his heart beat wildly in his chest.

The boy flailed in agony, blood from the bite spattering his arm and face as he spasmed. His twisting caught the rope between his body and the rugged cliff.

Agios, frantic to recover him, didn't realize that the knot was abrading until the rope snapped, with Philos not yet at the cliff top.

Agios screamed as he watched his son fall, his dark eyes locked on the child that was everything good, that held all the hope he had left in the world. He could do nothing.

Philos fell straight down to the lowest tree and smashed into it with an impact that surely ended his agony. His body hung there, broken and lifeless. After his first wail of pain he had not cried out again.

His son had died like a man.

It took Agios a day and part of a night to retrieve Philos's shattered body and take him back home. In their cabin Agios rested before leaving the warmth for the cool night. The wind, soft on the heels of the rain that had preceded it, filled the air with a scent so warm and rich, so full and verdant, that it seemed an affront, whispering slyly of living things, of flowers, leaves fresh and green. He held his breath.

From a lean-to shed behind the cabin, Agios took a homemade spade and pick and carried them to the top of a low rise not far away. All around the plateau the night lay soot-dark, but Agios had a hunter's vision and the stars sufficed for the work he had to do. A cairn of pale, smooth stones marked the grave of Philos's mother and stillborn younger brother. Near it Agios began to dig a second grave, difficult at first because of his weariness, and because he did not want to do this. His body was trying to refuse the errand. But Agios had no choice.

The rain had only slightly softened the soil and had not

penetrated very far. Agios swung the pick, chipped into the solid earth, moved to the side, and did it again, gradually chopping the hard ground into solid chunks that, with effort, he could pry loose and stack on one side of the grave.

His shoulder muscles clenched and tightened, and Agios began to sweat from the exertion. The rhythm of the pick and the burn in his arms was a relief, a pain that he could lean into.

Here in this shallow bowl of a mountainside glen, the soil had accumulated over the centuries. Some washed on down the slopes into the lower forests, into the fertile river valleys, but much of it remained here. It lay rich and dark. In the spring and summer it had yielded fruits and vegetables to supplement the meat he brought home. Agios was part hunter, part trapper, part farmer, part collector—all things he did well.

But now. *Now* what was he?

He pushed himself, not pausing to rest. He didn't realize he had fallen until the rocks began to dig into his knees. He welcomed the pain, something sharp and insistent that drew a little of the agony from his chest. He couldn't breathe. He couldn't see, and he blinked against the dark night and the tears that clouded his vision. The mountain cabin was solitary, but Agios was past caring if anyone could hear his sobs, the racking cry of an animal dying, of a shattered man.

He wanted to die.

He felt dead already.

By the time the sun rose, Agios was an empty husk. Some blood seeped into the ground beneath his legs and mixed with the dirt on his hands, but he didn't know if it was his blood or Philos's. The climb down the ravine and back up again with his broken son slung against his back had been a nightmare that no man should ever have to endure. Agios could still feel the slight weight between his shoulders, though Philos now lay wrapped beneath an olive tree less than two strides away.

Agios glanced at Philos's body and wished to see the slight rise and fall of his son's slender chest. But there was no undoing what had been done. The boy lay as still as stone, and just as cold. Morning burnished the marble skin of Philos's arm where it had fallen out from the folds of the cloak that Agios had wrapped him in. It was an outrage, a cruel joke that sunlight could make even this small portion of the child look so beautiful and whole. Agios scrambled over and tucked the slender arm back into the cloak. With a tenderness that belied the taut muscles of his forearms and the stern slant of his dark brows, he lifted the body. He did not look like a compassionate man, but he stepped into the grave he had dug and placed his son in the center as gently as a mother laying down her newborn.

"My son." His mouth formed the words, but Agios made no sound even though he tried again and again, his throat clenched with grief.

Still moving his lips, still groaning with the weight of all the yearning he couldn't voice, Agios touched the place where Philos's face was shrouded by the dusty cloak. It was a kind of blessing he offered in place of the words he could not say, a way to remember the feel of the boy's high cheekbones, the proud nose that he shared with Agios, and the fine mouth that was his mother's. It was good-bye.

The grave was small, but Agios bent his knees and back and lay beside Philos, his cheek in the grainy dirt and his hand resting on the body of his son. He wished he could have dug the grave larger, so large that he could creep into it with his boy and pull the earth in after them. He imagined dirt filling his nostrils, choking off the air, bringing death and peace—but how could he share the grave when he had allowed his own son to die?

No, he would leave his own bones elsewhere.

When Agios took up the spade and began to shovel the loose earth into the hole, his grief was already finding a new incarnation. He burned with sorrow, but the flames began to ignite a fury in his belly, an anger that grew with each spadeful of dirt. He filled in the grave and then lugged stones from the bed of a nearby stream with a strength that seemed inhuman after his loss and sleepless night.

He finished before the sun stood at noon. Agios looked at the fresh grave, the old grave, and the home that was no longer home, and then dragged his steps back into the cabin. Red embers of the fire still glared in the grate, and Agios blew them to life. He threw wood on, all the firewood left in the bin, and when that was gone the stools they had sat on, the short, crooked table he had made before becoming used to carpentry, and the olive-wood bowl his own hands had carved. What need did he have of these things now? Of the small bed he had shared with his wife? The pallet where his son had laid his head?

When the fire roared, he raked the burning coals out and scattered them across the floor. No vagabond would find the empty house and live there, where the memories of Weala and Philos and the nameless little baby deserved peace.

Agios didn't leave the cabin until it was a blaze that could be seen for miles, a funeral pyre. The smoke choked the sun-bright sky, belching a dark shadow over the mountain that spoke of evil things.

He left on foot with nothing in his hands. He didn't look back.

Agios had no destination, but he knew exactly what he wanted: oblivion. The village in the valley below his mountain home bustled with, if not friends, at least acquaintances. He didn't want to see them, didn't want them to ask about his son, and desired no commiseration or sympathy. He wished only to forget.

So he stuck to the mountain, following a path that he had worn smooth on his hunting trips, and walked along it until his legs would no longer carry him. Then, finding a crevice in a steep cliff, Agios pulled his cloak over his head and turned his back to the world. He didn't bother starting a fire because he didn't deserve warmth or protection. A part of him wished that he would never see another day, that the wolves who prowled the mountains would be hungry and bold.

Only a few short hours later, morning dawned crisp and gray, and Agios rolled over to face the faint light—still alive, whether he wanted to be or not, whether he believed he could bear it or not, weighted as he was with the burden of loss that hung like a stone in his chest.

Agios rose and kept walking because he didn't know what else to do. Grief moved him forward, away from the place where everything he had ever loved lay buried in the unforgiving ground. For two days he followed the mountain ridges until hunger and exhaustion drew him down to a village he had seen before but had never visited. He knew the kind of people who lived there, modest and hardworking famers, wary of strangers but slow to turn away someone in need.

The squat, square buildings of the humble homes stood pale in the afternoon sun, and white tendrils of smoke twisted lazily from cooking fires. His sandals skidded on the stones as he hiked down from the hill, but this was familiar land to Agios. Even half-starved and mad with grief, he was sure-footed.

It had been weeks since Agios had so much as spoken to anyone other than his son, and he approached the outskirts of the village reluctantly. The life he had carved out of the mountainside for himself and Philos was simple and solitary, but not lonely. Never lonely, for they'd had each other. But now the world seemed so barren and soulless that Agios wondered if he could trust his own mouth to form words. What was there to say?

In the end, he didn't have to say much at all. A girl who was drawing water from a well at the edge of the village pointed Agios in the direction of an inn before he even had the chance to ask. She also dipped a bowl into the cool, clean water and, with her eyes downcast, held it out to him. It was a customary offering, but Agios could tell it cost her effort. She was clearly shy in his presence. But that didn't stop him from drinking greedily, grateful for something other than the iron-flavored water he had sipped from trickling mountain springs.

"Thank you," he said gruffly, his voice thick and unfamiliar in his own ears. She nodded and backed away, and Agios left in the direction she had pointed.

The villagers weren't unfriendly, but they hurried by as he made his way through the narrow streets. If they knew what he had sewn into the hem of his cloak they would have treated him very differently, but Agios had no wish to be known as a trader in precious frankincense. That would mean questions, greedy eyes, and prying. He wanted only to buy food and to leave immediately.

He found the inn, but the woman who let him in shook her head and said, "No room."

"I can pay," Agios said, and pressed a small golden nugget into her hand. "Please. I'm hungry and thirsty, and I'm not well."

She looked doubtfully at his wild mane of black hair and his tangled beard and finally closed her hand on the offering. Without a word she went back into another room and soon returned holding a small bundle and an earthenware jar. "Here. Food. Drink," she said.

Agios accepted the provisions without complaint, even though he knew the nugget should have bought much more. He sat on the steps of the inn and drank a mouthful of the sour wine, then rose and walked on. He had no desire to bargain with the woman for a bed in the inn. At least he felt free as he strode away from the village.

The road ahead might be unknown, but it was better than the hum of chatter, the faint sound of laughter from behind a stone wall. Villagers had each other. Agios had no one.

He felt like a ghost, as if all that remained of the man he had been was a wisp of humanity so thin he hardly existed at all. But his belly still ached for food, and he finally stopped and unwrapped the five flat cakes he had bought from the woman at the inn. He ate two without noticing their taste, and a handful of the dry, salty olives that she had put in a small muslin bag. He ate none of the smoked fish, but he drank deeply from the earthenware jug of wine. He thought the taste was odd, sour yet bitter—perhaps the woman had added herbs because he had claimed to be ill. The warmth spreading down his throat and deep into his belly promised a deep and dreamless sleep.

Agios had not been drunk for years, and the stupor came

quickly. As his head fell back against the tree where he had paused to eat and drink, Agios felt momentarily grateful that he had at least avoided the main road. He should have climbed back into the mountains, but no matter. The sparse stand of pines a few miles from the village would do. The roads weren't safe, but he welcomed whatever the harsh and often deadly trade route had to offer. What could anyone take from him, after all, but his life?

Let them take it.

The days blurred into an endless weariness as Agios traveled on, never knowing or caring where his legs were taking him. But he couldn't outwalk memory, or the physical ache of his longing, or ease the feeling that something stronger than rope bound him to the mountain glen where he had buried his wife and sons. The cords drew tighter and tighter, a noose around his heart.

Agios dulled the pain with drink. Sometimes the homemade wine was premature and thin, the alcohol weak. Other times he could convince the merchant to lace it with something stronger. Occasionally the wine brought fleeting oblivion. A month went by, and then another, and still Agios could not sleep without wine—for if he tried, Philos came to him in dreams, silent but staring at him with reproachful eyes.

So Agios drank every night and woke every morning with wine still blurring his mind and pain throbbing in his temples. In a way, he wasn't at all surprised when one dawn he awakened to the cold sharp press of a spear point beneath his chin.

Fuzzy from sleep and still muddled by the contents of the empty jar beside him, Agios was nonetheless a fighter. The second the blade touched his skin he was awake, every nerve alive and flickering. *This*, he thought in the moment of first awareness, *this is what I've been waiting for*. He lay with eyes still closed, pretending to sleep on.

A man spoke, words in a language he did not know, and then in his own tongue someone else asked, "Is he alive?"

The first one, the one with the spear, grunted, and the second said, "Get him up."

Two men grabbed his arms and hauled him to his feet. He opened his eyes then and saw they were tall, well-muscled, and wearing leather armor.

The one with the spear stepped back and spat. With an unfamiliar accent, he said, "Still drunk. No threat."

It was nearly true, and Agios blearily looked around. Four men held him captive: the one with the spear, a shorter and older man in a sunset-colored robe who seemed to be in command, and the two armored guards who pinioned him. Beyond them—well, beyond them milled a crowd, men and camels and donkeys and three colossal gray beasts, a kind of animal he had never seen before.

"A caravan?" he asked, his tongue deliberately thick. He realized he was still too unsteady to fight well, and yet a part of him ached to fight. To die fighting.

The spearman said, "Let us kill him."

Agios felt the grip on his arms tighten.

"What did I do?" he demanded, making his voice more slurred than necessary. Could he fight, could he land a few blows that would make him feel he was striking back against the injustice that had stripped from his life everything good and beautiful?

His speaking had given them pause. The two men who flanked him looked dangerous and powerful, but they were bare-handed. The spearman, the one who had called for

21

his death, had rested his spear and had drawn a dagger and looked eager to use it—but the leader was holding up his hand, as if undecided.

Agios pretended to lose his footing, as if he were about to topple into unconsciousness, and the guard on his right shifted to support him. With a sudden twist, Agios wrenched his arm free and went for his own dagger.

"Watch him!" the older man warned, stepping back. The guards were good. They took his dagger before he had the chance to use it, but he struck hard with his fists, connecting more than once. He blacked one man's eye and bloodied another's nose, but the two guards took the blows, then wrestled him facedown to the ground and pressed him hard, twisting his arms in a painful lock.

"Go ahead," Agios said, hard gravel pressing into his cheek, his nose smarting as he breathed in dust. "Use your dagger."

But nothing came. No kick to the head or side, no angry cries calling for someone to spill his rebellious blood.

Then the older man said, "They will release you. Don't put up a fight. I have no wish to see you die."

The voice was close, and when they let Agios go, he rose to his hands and knees and saw the leader, whose face was sun-darkened and seamed like old leather, kneeling close to him. He held a faint smile on his face and a honeyed nugget of frankincense in his fingers. Agios realized with a start that it must have been dislodged from the folds of his robe.

"I want to ask you about this," the man said. "However"— he stood up—"I don't have the time at the moment, and you are still drunk. Later, then." He delivered the kick that Agios had been waiting for, and the world went dark.

Chapter 2

Agios woke to pain pulsing in his temple and bolting through his swollen jaw, but when he tried to lift a hand to assess the damage, he found that manacles and chains bound his wrists and ankles, and he lay in the dust with his tongue thickening in the heat of the day. His entire body ached for one sip of water. He raised his head and saw that he had been left on a heap of stone and dirt not far from the milling men and beasts of the caravan. His stomach muscles ached—they must have slung him over the back of an animal. He had a vague sense that they had traveled many miles since he had been kicked unconscious.

Why were they keeping him alive?

No guard stood over him. Probably they thought him harmless, chained as he was. *That might work to my advantage*, he thought.

Some distance away a dozen or more of the brightly dressed members of the caravan reclined in the shade of some roadside acacia trees, but a smaller group had clustered around one of the hulking gray animals. The creature stood patiently as the men yammered and gestured over—something—that lay in pieces on the ground. "Never seen such a thing, barbarian? The beast comes from India. It's called an elephant."

Agios hadn't realized that someone had come up behind him. Twisting around, he saw the speaker—one of the two heavyset guards, the one with the black eye. He sat on some kind of folded pad, just out of arm's reach, holding a dagger and idly scratching at the soil with the tip.

"I'm supposed to keep you alive," the man said with a grin. "If I had my own way, I'd gut you." With the dagger point he flicked a pebble. Agios twitched away, taking it on the cheek instead of in the eye.

"Do it, then," Agios said.

"Can't. You have something they want."

The frankincense. Wherever it grew, some ruler claimed it—and men who did not recognize any king or emperor took it. That was why he had kept the location of the grove he had discovered secret, why he had put adders there to guard it. He had spread tales among traders, too, of curses and demonic serpents that protected any libanos tree. "I had one piece of it," Agios said, his throat so parched his voice rasped.

The guard rose and took the folded pad from beneath him. It was Agios's cloak, ripped to pieces, all the hidden pockets cut open. All the frankincense was gone. "You're no merchant," the guard said. "You know where it grows. We want more."

Agios said, "You took all I had."

"But you know where there is more. My masters want you to gather it for them."

"If I do this for you?" Agios whispered.

"I can't understand you."

"Dry," Agios croaked.

The man reached beneath his robes and produced a leather wineskin. "Open your mouth, barbarian."

Agios rolled onto his back, and the guard opened the wineskin and let a thin warm stream—water, not wine—flow. It splattered on Agios's forehead before finally, blessedly, it found his mouth. He gulped until the guard tilted the wineskin, cutting off the flow. "Better?"

Agios nodded. "If I do what your masters want, what will I get for it?"

The guard shrugged. "We might let you live."

The squabbling men near the elephant raised their voices in a furious gabble. Agios did not recognize their language.

"What are they angry about?"

The guard glanced over. "An accident. The howdah is destroyed. They are blaming each other."

"Howdah?"

"A—like a—it's a platform the elephant carries—a barbarian wouldn't understand."

"I am good with my hands. I have been a woodcarver and carpenter. Let me have a look. Maybe I can help."

The guard walked away, toward a tent. A few moments later he came back. "I'm told you can look at it. Come." He leaned down, grasped the chain linking the manacles, and with easy strength pulled Agios to his feet. "Can you stand?"

Agios stood unsteadily. He was sober now, but cramped and aching, and the chains that bound his ankles together shortened his step. The guard steadied him by the arm as he shuffled toward the elephant. "You were the one who tried to catch me when I fell," Agios said.

The guard grunted. "If I had known how hard you could hit, I wouldn't have bothered."

The quarreling men, faces red with rage, fell sullenly silent as they approached. The guard spoke to them in their language, they complained, but then one of them led a second elephant over, one with a howdah still girthed onto its broad back. Agios studied it and the broken pieces of the one that had been shattered. It looked beyond repair.

Agios squatted to examine the splintered ruin and then stood and looked again at the intact howdah. "Could they take that one off so I can see it better?"

Again the guard spoke, again the men complained, but they had the elephant kneel. Agios put out his chained hands to feel the hot, leathery skin, wondering at the bulk of the animal. He realized that the damage looked much worse than it actually was and said slowly, "I think I can repair this."

One of the elephant drivers snorted and said in Agios's language, "This uncouth being is insolent. Is he a man? Does he have a name?"

"Agios," he said, standing over the broken howdah and noting what would be needed.

"Agios," said the guard, pronouncing it *AH-gee-ohs*.

"*Ah-GEE-ohs*," Agios corrected. "It's my name. At least say it right."

The guard laughed. "Agios," he said, struggling with the word but coming close. "Lord Agios of the Frankincense. Tell these men what you can do."

"Well, to begin with I will have to find some good hard wood. And then I'll need tools—you probably have what I need." Agios knelt and pointed, explaining what he would do to repair the howdah. The men grew interested.

When Agios finished, one of the men said eagerly to the guard, "Let him do this. I will pay you if he can repair it. Without it, I'll lose a third of my profit! What is he, a slave?"

"Captive," the guard said. He turned to Agios. "My master said to let you do what you could. Tell these men what tools you need."

Agios recited the list: saw, auger, a hammer, an awl for the leather, a knife. The elephant's owner sent a man running to fetch them. Agios held up his wrists, the chain jangling. "Remove these."

The guard shook his head. "You can work with them on."

"I can't," Agios said. "Leave on the leg shackles, but I need both hands."

"I'd like to see what he can do," a voice said from behind

them. Agios saw it was the man in the red robe. "Release him from his bonds, Gamos. You have complained about his hitting you. You may guard him and use what force you like to prevent him from escaping."

Gamos bowed and unbolted the wristlets. "I will have to find wood," Agios told the man in the robe.

"If I swear to you that you will not be harmed by any of us, will you in turn swear to return here after finding what you need?"

"I swear it."

"Go with him, Gamos. If he does anything he shouldn't, hurt him." The man smiled without real humor. "I don't distrust your oath, Agios, but I'm no fool, either."

Agios did not respond, but noticed the man at least pronounced his name correctly.

He and Gamos left the trail together and walked a few miles to a forest standing in the foothills. Gamos carried his spear, but Agios wouldn't have tried to run even without the threat of being impaled. He had always been like that when a job lay before him: he did what had to be done, and then moved on to the next thing.

They didn't speak much, but at one point Gamos said, "You're a strong man. And quick. I didn't expect that blow."

"You thought I was drunk," Agios said. "That gave me an advantage."

"Not much of one," Gamos said.

"No," Agios admitted. "I *was* pretty drunk."

They reached the trees, stunted ones in this arid countryside, and although Agios did not recognize them, he found some that reminded him of white acacia. Gamos didn't know what the trees were, either, but they found one that had fallen and had not rotted. Agios had carried a leather pouch with tools inside. He took out a saw and cut the trunk into manageable pieces, roughing out boards large enough for his purposes.

The sun had sunk low when he and Gamos returned to the encamped caravan. Agios put down the wood and the tools and asked for food—he was ravenous—and water. They brought him bread and dried goat's flesh, and he ate. "Now let me work," he said.

He ran his hands over the pieces of the howdah. Agios loved the feel and texture of wood, and he saw that he could salvage nearly all of the broken device. He removed three crucial pieces, fitted them together, and used them as a pattern.

Night fell and he worked by torchlight, carving the replacement pieces. He liked the unfamiliar wood: with its fine dense grain, it shaped well, and it had a springy strength and a pleasing spicy scent. He ignored the onlookers—none of them seemed to want to go to bed—until, when it was nearly midnight, he secured the new pieces into place.

The owner of the elephant inspected it, clapped his hands, and said, "Ah!"

The animal's handlers deftly restrung the straps and harnesses and replaced the split girth with another length of leather. The animal knelt, they placed the howdah on the beast's back, cinched and fastened it. And then, the elephant rose—wondrous! Both animal and its burden looked as good as new. The elephant's owner made an elaborate speech, punctuated with gestures, none of which Agios understood.

After a long time, when the man had finally finished, Gamos said drily, "He thanks you." Then he added, "And he says you stink."

They had crossed a small stream during their excursion to find wood, and the next morning Gamos took Agios back there to bathe. The had reached a tentative understanding while Agios had worked on the howdah, so Gamos stood guard casually as Agios stripped and stepped into the waist-high water. However, Gamos still kept one hand on his spear and the other near the hilt of his dagger.

Agios didn't care. The cool water seemed to return him fully to himself. Grief was still a phantom that clung to his shoulders, but the wine was finally gone from his head. He wondered what it would be like to return to his mountain, to visit the graves, and the thought stabbed into him. He scooped up sand from the riverbed and used it to scrub his skin until it was red and raw. Then Agios dipped beneath the water and ran his hands through the tangle of his hair and his long beard.

They walked back to the caravan without speaking, but Agios sensed that Gamos was thinking carefully about something the entire way.

"Am I to be chained again?" Agios asked when they were near the road. He held out his arms as if welcoming the possibility, but Gamos took one look at his bloodied wrists and shook his head.

"If you run I'll hunt you down."

"I won't run."

"I know."

The caravan was already on the move. They traveled until nearly sunset, when they camped again beside the track. Some erected tents, others spread blankets on the ground. Now that they didn't hang back from him, Agios saw that some women were among the men. "No prostitutes," Gamos told him with a sad shake of his head. "These are wives. A caravan takes years to go, years to return. Sometimes children are born along the way. By the time they return home with their parents they can walk on their own."

Agios tried to close his heart and his mind to the memory of Philos's birth. Those early years when his son was as fragile as a bird and just about as big. The day he first toddled across the cabin floor. How Philos would have loved to see the elephants!

Soon, Agios thought as pain stabbed through him. *My son, I'll find death soon.*

Agios's father had taught him that after death, men's spirits lived on. He had never seen a spirit and did not much believe in them—but if he could see his son again, and his wife—

No, let me stop thinking.

Gamos mistook Agios's solemnity for hunger and motioned for him to sit near a fire where a leg of mutton was turning slowly on a spit. "I'd starve you," Gamos told him cheerfully, "but then you might not be able to complete your task."

"And what is my task?"

"To gather the frankincense, of course."

If I don't tell them where I gather it, Agios thought, *they will keep me alive*. "Who wants it so badly?"

As Gamos considered the question, a woman came, carrying a flat board with the roasted mutton steaming on it. Gamos took out his dagger and cut off two pieces. He handed the smaller portion over slowly, as if he was still deciding whether Agios deserved food. "It's to be a gift," he said finally, and for a moment Agios wasn't sure if he was talking about the mutton or the frankincense. "A gift for a king."

"Can't a king buy his own frankincense?" Agios tore off a hunk of meat and tried to eat it slowly, even though his stomach was hollow and aching.

Gamos grinned and grease trickled into his beard. "Not this one. He is newly born. Or soon will be."

Before he could say more, someone in camp shouted

frantically. In an instant, Gamos sprang to his feet, dropping his share of mutton. "Bandits!"

He seized his spear, but Agios also leaped up and grabbed Gamos's arm roughly. "You can't leave me unarmed."

Gamos gave Agios a hard look, reached into his belt, and yanked out the dagger, then handed it to Agios blade first. It was a warning, and as Agios reached past the glinting iron to grip the hilt, their hands touched in a silent covenant. Agios wouldn't run and Gamos knew it.

Throwing himself into the shadows, Agios stumbled over a fallen body. Six or eight men off in the darkness loosed arrows into the camp. One whiffed so close that Agios felt the wind of its flight. People from the caravan were massing to charge into the dark.

Agios realized that the archers were far too few to take on a caravan of thirty men. He saw the silhouette of Gamos against the torchlight and shouted, "This has to be a diversion! Don't let them be pulled away from the tents!"

Wasting no time, Gamos called out sharply in at least two languages. The caravan guards heard and fell back. A woman screamed from the far side of the camp. Agios raced there, leaping over a campfire, his heart pumping.

A tent had caught fire, and in the flaring light Agios saw

a dozen or more men, wearing leather armor and armed with spears and short swords, hacking at the faltering defenders.

Roaring, Agios threw himself into the fight. A spearman, startled at his onslaught, spun as Agios knocked him down, grasped the spear, reversed it, and battered down another attacker, hitting him hard in the center of his chest. Still another swung a vicious sword, but Agios spun, got the spear haft between the swordsman's legs, and swept him off his feet. The man lost his weapon as he fell and flung out his hands, trying to catch himself.

Agios seized the sword. He dived low, hamstrung one bandit, tripped another, and clubbed him with the butt of the spear. People shouted. Agios heard men and women screaming. A huge brute of an attacker bore down on him, and Agios dropped backward, braced his spear, and caught him in the stomach. The dying man fell on him, a ponderous weight reeking of sweat. Agios grunted as he rolled him off, got back to his feet, and found the battle had ended.

Gamos shouted, others answered him. Torches flared, and bandits turned and fled in the sudden light. Agios heard the twang of bowstrings and saw two more of the robbers go down, struck from behind as they ran. Then the survivors had fled into darkness.

Two members of the caravan rushed to threaten Agios with spears. If they recognized him, they believed he belonged in chains. Agios dropped the curved sword and held up his hands. "Gamos!" he shouted.

The guard came at once, spoke severely to the spearmen, and then grasped Agios's arm as he loudly proclaimed something.

The spearmen bowed and murmured. "What did you tell them?" Agios asked.

"That you saved us all."

"I didn't. I only helped."

"Sometimes a little help is all one needs to be saved," Gamos said, studying him thoughtfully. He seemed to decide something. "Come. We'll treat that wound."

The pain had not hit him until then—Agios had not even felt the bite of the arrow that had pierced the meat of his left thigh. Gamos saw to it, warning Agios that he would feel even more pain. The arrow had almost but not quite made its way out again, and Gamos had to push it through the skin—that would cause less damage than trying to pull the barbs out through the muscle.

Agios lay on his side, watching as Gamos manipulated the arrow. The arrowhead made a tented shape under his skin, then came through with a bright burst of blood.

Gamos cut the shaft just behind the head and pulled it out—that felt worse than the other had.

"You have been a soldier," Gamos murmured.

"No. Never."

"Then you stand pain well." Applying some poultice, Gamos bandaged the leg. "I think that will do," he said. "It only caught the outside edge of your leg. Fortunately, the robbers around here do not poison their arrows."

"Thank you. I wounded you," Agios said. "And you healed me."

Gamos laughed at that. "A lie. There were two of us and one of you. We subdued you easily, and a bruise is not a wound." But the tight skin beneath his swollen eye glinted black in the firelight.

A man, one of the young guards, came up and said something to Gamos. He spoke back, the man nodded, and then the guard ran off again. "We lost one sentinel," Gamos said. "We have five wounded, six counting you, though none serious enough to delay us. The bandits lost seven men. You wounded three more."

"Badly?" Agios asked. He heard a scream.

"Not badly enough," Gamos said.

Agios frowned. "You're having them killed?"

Gamos smiled grimly. "If a serpent struck at you, would you kill it?"

Agios had no answer for that.

Chapter 3

A gios knew the members of the caravan looked on him as an enigma, a drunken prisoner destined to be killed casually on the roadside who'd saved his own life by proving useful. They wondered about him but kept their distance—Gamos the guard was always at his side, and who knew when Agios might fall from favor again? As for Gamos, he had begun to treat Agios not with friendship, but with a kind of grudging respect, as if they were distant relatives in a squabbling family.

The elephants separated from the rest of the caravan, traveling eastward to the Mediterranean ports where the Roman trading fleets came to load precious cargo from the east, spices, silks, and exotic animals. The rest of the travelers, who had been heading north, now turned gradually toward the east. A day came when they skirted mountains that resembled those of Agios's homeland so much that they made him think of Philos.

"What is it?" Gamos asked as Agios stared into the distance.

"Nothing."

"Why do these mountains fill you with sorrow?"

Agios didn't look at him. "Not the mountains. Memories."

"Ah," Gamos said. "You have lost someone. A brother? Parents? A woman?"

"It doesn't matter," Agios said gruffly.

"I've lost good friends," Gamos said. "In battle. It hurts. Talking might help."

Agios remained silent for many strides.

Gamos eventually said, "Some religions teach that after we die our spirits live on in a kingdom underground. I have hopes of seeing my friends again."

"I don't know about any of that," Agios said heavily. "Maybe they do go on. Sometimes I see them in my dreams."

He would say no more.

The journey to the northeast was a slow one, and the seasons began to change, the last of summer fading in dry heat. Half a year had passed since the ravine, and more months might go by before they reached their journey's end. Agios didn't care. The slow progress of the caravan kept his mind from other things. They passed far beyond the lands of desert and came to places lush with growing things.

And it was beautiful. The mountains were soft and green, for it was the end of the monsoon season and the earth burgeoned with growth. The road-weary travelers walked with more spring in their step.

Gamos said, "If my master is true to the rendezvous, we should meet him in a very few days."

"And who is this master?" Agios asked.

"A ruler who is both powerful and wise. A man of thought as well as action. His name is Caspar, and he's a very well-known scholar. He speaks many languages, and reads them as well."

The two guards and their commander, the man in the red robes, whose name was Mizha, left the caravan in a harbor city. They traveled inland for five more days before coming to a town. It did not seem to be a capital city, nor was the building they approached a palace, though it did look substantial and rich.

They entered a courtyard and then a room full of scrolls, where a dark man sat at a table. Agios noticed the bright fabric of his clothes, the rich dyes being a sign of wealth. The man stood as Gamos and the others bowed to him. Agios judged him to be forty-five or fifty, a lean, trim figure whose hair and beard were iron-gray. He asked Gamos a question in his native language—in the many weeks on the road, Agios had learned enough of it from Gamos to catch the gist: "Is this the man the messengers brought word of?"

Mizha said, "Yes, my lord. He had this."

And he unfolded the cloak that had hidden the riches. Even now the fragrance of frankincense wafted from it. Agios bowed his head, tears stinging his eyes. The aroma brought back that terrible day so clearly, brought back Philos as he had been just before—

Caspar had spoken to him in his own language. Agios forced his mind back to the present. "I'm sorry. I didn't—"

"I asked your name."

"Agios," he said.

"I am Caspar. My kingdom is to the south, but I have

come here because the man who owns this mansion has collected all these." He waved his hands toward the scrolls. "Do you know why we want you?"

"Frankincense," Agios said. "I have heard it's a gift for a king—a king not yet born."

"Leave us," Caspar said to the others.

"My lord," Mizha said in a tone of reproach, "he is a barbarian."

"Are you going to kill me, Agios?" Caspar asked.

"No."

"There. I'm safe. Go on."

The others left reluctantly. Caspar beckoned Agios over to the table. "Do you read?"

"I have not the skill," Agios said.

"It is a useful knowledge."

He does not plan to kill me, Agios thought. He said, "Your men probably have told you that you can't threaten me with death. I don't care whether I live or die. But to be able to read—that would be good. I will help you if you teach me that skill."

Caspar looked at him as if seeing him for the first time. "You won't try to escape?"

"No. I swear it."

45

"Then I will have a servant teach you." Caspar reached for some scrolls. "Here, these are star charts—you see? These others are ancient prophecies. They speak of a king to come, and my study of the sky tells me the time of his coming is upon us."

"What do you see in the sky?"

"I hope—I fervently long—to see a star that will be the sign of his birth," Caspar said.

Agios did not really understand, but replied, "What is another king? There are kings everywhere."

Caspar's eye glinted. "This shall be the King of Kings."

Agios had no reply.

"They tell me you can secure more frankincense?" Caspar made the statement a question, the matter clearly of great import to him.

"Yes, in my homeland. There is a place that will offer it in abundance now. It has not been gathered for a year. The trees will be heavy with it."

I'd meant for Philos to have a harvest to make him proud.

Caspar asked him where his homeland was, and when he told, as best he could, the king shook his head. "It is difficult to trade for frankincense—so many wealthy men and such high prices. But I need a great deal it, and if it is available in your homeland—well, it is a long way back there. However, for the longest part of the journey we will go by sea. Not too far from where you say the frankincense is, there is another kingdom where a friend of mine lives—his name is Balthasar, and he also looks for the coming of the King of Kings. Before I join Balthasar to find the new king, though, we must also travel to meet another scholar-king. His name is Melchior. You will meet them both before they and I depart on our search. I will have new garments readied for you. We will leave in two days."

The ship moved faster than men mounted or walking on foot, but it hugged the coastline and the trip back took weeks. A servant, and sometimes Caspar himself, taught Agios some rudiments of reading and writing on the way. He also observed that Agios had a gift for picking up languages. He tutored Agios in Aramaic, a tongue used by traders throughout that part of the world, and by the time they reached port Agios could hold a halting conversation in that language.

They joined yet another caravan, and Agios soon settled

back into the routine. The days were long and hot, but the people seemed in good spirits, and in the evenings they sometimes sang songs in exotic tongues and danced around the fire. Gamos had made a gift of the woodworking tools that Agios had used to repair the howdah. As a result, Agios had taken up carving again. It wasn't a conscious decision. One night he found himself handling a chunk of wood, the knife flashing in the firelight. He had passed the long evening hours like this when Philos was a child, and though it had been years since he had fashioned likenesses with nothing more than a knife and a piece of wood, he still had the knack.

A goat was the first thing to take shape beneath his able fingers, and though it wasn't as precise as he would have liked, the horns were tiny and sharp and the hooves cloven. He practiced next on a leopard. Then a bird with wings outstretched and an elephant. The animals got better every time.

Agios didn't know what to do with the carvings and he didn't dare to approach any of the children in the caravan— the eyes of young boys and girls always brought a stabbing memory of Philos. So he left his homemade gifts in unexpected places where they would surprise and delight whoever found them. Only Gamos knew that Agios had carved the sheep that a woman then found balanced on the edge of her cooking pot. And they shared a smile over the sharp-eyed hawk that perched in a net as a small boy spent the better portion of a day trying to devise ways to reach it.

One evening some strangers joined the caravan, four men who led a fifth one, a hulking fellow whose arms were tightly bound by leather thongs. Gamos saw them first and spoke with them, then came to where Agios sat outside Caspar's tent. "These men claim they've captured a demon. He's ugly enough to be one."

The bound man's groans came to them. Agios rose and walked over to look more closely. The bound man was hideous: hair matted, limbs knotted and gnarled despite their apparent strength. His eyes were wild, widely spaced, and too small. The brute glared around and grunted.

"What's wrong with him?" Agios asked.

One of the man's captors shrugged. "He's like an animal. A Roman got him in Cyprus, they say, and made him a galley slave, but he could learn nothing, not even how to row. The Romans sold him to us, and we use him like a donkey—he can carry heavy loads. But he's disobedient and tries to run away. We hope to sell him to someone who needs a slave with muscles and no mind."

Agios stared at the prisoner, and for just a moment their gazes locked. The expression on the man's face was one of utter hopelessness. "He's no demon," Agios muttered. "Just miserable and exhausted and frightened."

That evening when he lay waiting for sleep, Agios felt unsettled. He was sure that he could hear the moaning of the bound man at the farthest edge of the camp, and the hopeless groans pieced his heart. Why should he care? But there was something in the monster's eyes that haunted him.

A dark mist of dust surrounded the caravan as a wind storm rolled in across the mountains. Agios slept fitfully, half-awake as he watched the shadows disperse and then coalesce into dark and menacing shapes. Murmurs rose all around, muttering threats and wickedness until Agios lay covered in a cold and terrified sweat.

And then, through the darkness, a spot of light began to glow like a white-hot coal in the distance. Agios tried to walk toward it, but in his half dream it receded before him. He thought at first that it was a star. Maybe Caspar's star, the very one he longed to find.

But then, somehow, Agios was closer. It wasn't a star at all, but a room. And the room wasn't in a house, but in a cave carved into the side of a hill, and warm light poured from it into the black night outside. Agios tried to approach the door—he was suddenly anxious to see inside. But he couldn't. There was only the light and a feeling like a feather in his chest, a feeling that maybe the darkness might not be as terrible as he believed it to be.

Hope.

The word had been whispered to his heart, and despite all that he had lost, despite all of the pain that he carried around like shackles even more real than the ones that had left scars on his wrists, Agios longed to believe hope might exist for him.

But as quickly as it had come, the light vanished.

And the whisper of hope with it.

Agios woke on the cold, hard ground and knew that he had nothing to live for.

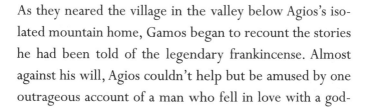

As they neared the village in the valley below Agios's isolated mountain home, Gamos began to recount the stories he had been told of the legendary frankincense. Almost against his will, Agios couldn't help but be amused by one outrageous account of a man who fell in love with a goddess. He tried to climb a steep cliff to find her, but was cursed and transformed into a tree that could only grow on nearly vertical stone. His tears crystallized into the frankincense resin.

"You believe this?" Agios asked.

"You don't?"

Agios shrugged.

"Caspar says the Hebrew God created and consecrated the libanos tree," Gamos said.

"Why?"

"So frankincense could be used to cleanse and sanctify temples sacred to him."

"I know nothing about the Hebrew God."

"Come on." Gamos wouldn't be deterred. "Surely you believe in something. All right, you know the truth about this plant. Tell me about the dangers of frankincense."

"Deadly serpents guard the trees," Agios said after a long moment.

Gamos looked skeptical. "You mean dragons?"

"I don't know what those are. These—their bite burns like flame."

"Dragons, then. Winged serpents that fly and breathe fire," Gamos said, sounding skeptical.

"Serpents, anyway," Agios said. "But aside from them, we must be careful. People covet frankincense. If they suspect we have any, look for trouble—they wouldn't hesitate to kill for it."

On the morning when Caspar and his small band prepared to leave the caravan, Agios heard sounds of pain. He turned and headed for them. Gamos asked, "Where are you going?" and followed close behind.

The owners of the misshapen slave were whipping him. The man had been bound to a cartwheel, his back stripped bare, and the four laid into him with short, viciously knotted scourges. The bound man shrieked as the braided knots cut bloody stripes into his flesh.

Agios grabbed the uplifted arm of the leader, wrenched the scourge from his grasp, and turned. The others fell back. "You'll kill him!" Agios said.

"What if we do?" the leader snarled. "He tried to get loose again. What good is he to us? Who would buy this filth?"

The bound man whimpered and tried to speak, but his words were a gabble.

Agios turned to Gamos. "Buy him."

"What?"

"He's strong. Buy him."

"That's insane."

"You took my frankincense," Agios said. "You owe me. Buy this man."

Caspar came finally. When Agios repeated his demand, the king looked doubtfully at the weeping, bound figure. "What need have I of a servant like this? This is a strange thing to ask."

Agios said, "You want something from me. I want this from you." He glared at the four men who had been whipping the slave. "They will take one silver piece."

The leader began to protest, but glancing at Agios's face he broke off and muttered, "That will do."

And so they left that morning with the extra man. As they walked away, one of the four men yelled after them: "His name's Krampus. He'll kill you in the night unless you tie him up!"

Krampus, bent and cringing, edged closer to Agios. Agios didn't look at him but said, "I won't tie you up. No one will beat you."

Krampus wept and reached out a hand to touch Agios's shoulder tentatively. He made placating sounds, like a dog. Then, with the gentleness of a child, he took Agios's pack and bag of tools from him. For the rest of that day they walked side by side.

They bypassed the village and Agios led them along the trail that took them first to the mountain glen where the blackened ash-mound and the two stone cairns waited—Agios giving no sign that they meant anything to him—and then along the great ridge that took them to the plateau cut by the ravine. They reached it at sunset and camped there.

Caspar asked, "Is this the place?"

Agios nodded. "Tomorrow I'll gather the frankincense—if some other collector has not found the grove."

"I need enough to fill a vessel of one sacred *mina*," the scholar-king said. When Agios did not respond, he explained, "About twice the volume of an ordinary wine cup. That would be a gift worthy of the greatest of kings."

"And how much was in my garment that Gamos took from me?" Agios asked.

"Perhaps a twelfth of what I need." Caspar bowed his head. "I will recompense you for it. I did not mean for my men to steal."

But you didn't offer to return it, Agios thought. He watched Caspar as he touched the leather sack that he kept tied to his belt.

Krampus had not tried to escape, not once, and when he had been cleaned up and dressed in decent clothing, he no longer looked like a monster, but simply like an unfortunately ugly man. He could speak—not clearly—but could ask "Food? Water?" when he hungered or thirsted. And he could say "Agios."

When the dawn came, Agios said, "Let Krampus come with me. There are dangers ahead. You'll be able to see us from here. If trouble comes, I'll call out. We will need a rope."

"I'll go with you," Gamos said.

"If you want."

At first Krampus shrank from the rope, perhaps thinking he was to be tied again, but Agios showed him what he had to do—to stand with the rope wound around him and to let the slack out gradually as Agios descended the cliff. The man was strong. It was like clinging to a rope lashed to a stone pillar.

They bypassed the first two trees—the ones that Agios and Philos had already harvested—and came to one that grew so high on the cliff that, lying on his stomach, Agios could almost reach the top branches. He stretched out and squinted down at it and the libanos trees below, trying to see if the resin still clung there or if it had become too heavy and fallen. Enough of it gleamed dully to tell Agios that he could collect an amount from the trees that would satisfy Caspar.

"Doesn't look too hard," Gamos said from beside him. The man had joined Agios on his stomach and as he spoke he stretched out his arm. One of the branches coiled and struck.

Agios knocked Gamos's arm away just in time. The serpent had barely missed him. It recoiled, looping its body around a branch, and hissed.

"Adders," Agios warned. "Their bite is deadly."

"By the gods!" Gamos muttered. "There are scores of them! What do they live on?"

"Birds. Small animals."

"How did they get here?"

Bitterly, Agios said, "I put them here myself."

He had brought a long pole, and he dislodged the first snake with it. The adder tumbled down, landing in a lower tree, where more snakes hissed and squirmed. Agios probed, but the highest tree held no more threat. "I'm going down," Agios said. He made sure his short knife hung secure in its sheath at his belt. Before taking up the rope, he said, "You've been kind enough to me, Gamos. If I should die here, take care of this man Krampus. See that he's not mistreated."

"I'll do my best."

"Help him hold the rope. This is slow work."

Krampus spread his legs and braced himself, the rope wound around his waist. Gamos took up the slack and stood ready to pay it out as Agios descended. Agios swung over the edge, braced his feet against the stone, and let himself down. The first tree only had a few nuggets of resin—the rest must have grown too dry and heavy and fallen to the valley below. Finding the remaining bits was a tedious job, and the strain of holding on to the rope made his shoulders ache, but Agios gathered the precious resin one-handed, storing it in a cloth bag slung to his belt.

He moved to the next lower tree. An adder looped around a low branch, and Agios moved very, very slowly as he cleared the higher ones. The snake suddenly struck, lightning-fast. Agios swiveled and caught it just behind the head. The furious serpent thrashed and hissed as he dropped it. It fell a long way down and died on the tumbled rocks below.

Agios's eyes stung with sweat. He worked as quickly as he could and cleared that tree, then another and another.

"I have it," he called at last. They pulled him up until again he reached the highest tree. "Wait. Let me rest a while. I'll throw the bag to you before coming up." With the rope taking most of his weight, he put his feet on the sturdiest branches of the tree and got ready to toss the pouch. Once that was done, it would be the work of a moment to pull his knife and cut through the rope. He would fall as Philos had fallen. He locked his jaw tightly. He would die, as Philos had, without a cry.

But as Agios drew back his arm to throw the sack of resin, something stopped him. A heart-wrenching wail came from the cliff top—his name, slurred and changed into a child's frantic plea for a parent. Krampus, who must be afraid for him.

"Throw it!" Gamos said. "I don't know if he'll hold on much longer—I don't think he understands. Throw it and come up!"

Krampus wailed again, and the rope felt as if the rescued slave were edging toward the cliff. Agios nearly lost his footing.

GLENN BECK

Gamos cried out furiously, "Get back! If you let him fall, I'll kill you!"

Krampus was yowling. What would happen to him if Agios let himself die? Pity moved Agios's heart, and he shouted, "Caspar! Caspar the Scholar!"

For a few moments there was nothing, and then Agios could see Caspar himself peeking over the side of the cliff.

"Do you have it?" Caspar asked.

"You know I do."

"Throw it to me."

"No," Agios shouted back. "I want something from you."

Caspar's eyes narrowed. "Your life is in my hands, friend."

"My life means nothing to me."

"Then what do you want?"

"Krampus."

"What? This slave I bought?" Even at a distance, Agios could tell that Caspar was confused. "What do you want with him?"

"You don't want him! You said so. One silver piece wouldn't have bought a twentieth of the frankincense you took from me. Now I've gathered this." Agios held the bag

60

out. "Sell Krampus to me for what you took and for what I've done!"

Caspar stared at him, his lips pressed together shrewdly. "Tell me if you mean to harm him."

"I intend to free him."

Caspar's eyes went wide with surprise. "Then you are a better man than I had hoped." Caspar nodded firmly. "He is yours."

"Swear it to me."

"I swear it."

Agios could feel a tug on the rope as Gamos began to haul hand over hand. When he reached the lip of the gorge, he threw the sack at Caspar's chest. He strode to Krampus and took the rope from him. "I'm back. You did well. Come."

Caspar's party walked all the rest of that day and into the night before they came again to the village. Two watchmen there let them enter the place—but one said, "Not this ugly brute." He threatened Krampus with the point of a spear. Fury rose in Agios, and in one outraged movement he jerked the spear from the guard's hands and thrust the shaft hard against his throat. The man fell, sputtering, and Agios whipped around to face the second. He had his spear trained on Krampus and wasn't expecting the punishing blow to his knees as Agios used the weapon like a club.

"If you ever touch him again, I'll kill you." Agios spat, standing over the wounded, uncomprehending men. Then he snapped the shaft of the spear over his knee and tossed the broken pieces at them.

Turning to Krampus, Agios looked him full in the eye. He wasn't sure if the giant could understand, but it didn't matter. "You and I will camp outside the village. Come," Agios said. And Krampus followed.

Chapter 4

I loathed how his owners treated that poor man," Caspar told Agios after they had left the mountain and caught up to the caravan.

"If you didn't like it, why didn't you do something about it?" Agios asked. They were reclining in Caspar's tent, enjoying a light meal of honeyed cakes and figs from the groves near the base of the mountains. For all his size and clumsiness, Krampus ate very carefully, pulling off small pieces of the dense cake and then licking every crumb from his thick fingers. He stole the occasional glance at Agios, and each time Agios took time himself to smile a little. He wanted the big man to know that he meant no harm.

Caspar said, "I am not king here. And I am not a soldier." He spread his hands, revealing palms soft and unlined, the hands of a man unaccustomed to heavy physical labor or the heft of a sword.

Agios didn't say anything, and Caspar clapped, ending the conversation. "Shall we see if we have met our mark?"

A servant hurried over and measured the frankincense in an ornate bronze cup. When the man nodded and reported, "More than full measure, sir," the scholar smiled and glanced at Agios.

Agios returned his gaze. Beside him Krampus stirred restlessly. The flaps of the tent had been closed and it was getting hot and stuffy. At length, Caspar said, "You have done well, Agios. What compensation would please you?"

"Proof that Krampus is mine. You sold him to me, remember?"

"Of course," Caspar replied. He whispered something to the servant, who disappeared through a fold in the tent. Moments later a scribe appeared. The scribe handed Caspar a square of paper—the rare Egyptian invention made of pressed reeds. "Here is his document. It says he belongs to you." The scribe melted wax, and Caspar pressed his ring into the cooling surface. "I have sealed it with my own impression."

Agios accepted the paper and rose. He motioned that Krampus should also stand, and the strong man scrambled up awkwardly, as though unused to having no fetters on wrists and ankles. Others in the caravan had demanded that Krampus be restrained, but Agios had prevailed. By now the merchants knew of Agios's skill, and they heard whispers that he had done a great service for a king. He was a hero of sorts, but he longed to be away from the press of people and their prying eyes.

Agios bowed his head, trying to find a word of farewell. He had not expected to return, had thought he would die on the mountain, but in accepting responsibility for the deformed slave, he had somehow tied himself to life again. But though Krampus would never again feel the bite of a whip, how were they to live—and where? Agios had no plans, and he hesitated.

Caspar had risen, too. "Of course you are free to go," he said, as if sensing Agios's inner uncertainty. "However, I feel you have paid far too much for this slave's freedom. I am still in your debt, Agios, and I wish to reward you further. Now, tedious journeys still lie ahead for me. I wonder— would you accept service for a while longer?"

"I serve no man," Agios said.

Caspar raised his hand. "Don't be so hasty. As I told you, I have two friends, scholars like me, who are joining me on a journey to where the new king will be found. Like me, they will carry precious gifts. We have no wish to travel in full panoply, with an army accompanying us, but in ordinary clothing, with only a few servants. Yet, with riches in our baggage, we need protection. You and your big friend—"

"His name is Krampus," Agios said.

Caspar nodded gravely. "Very well. You and Krampus could act as our guards. You are cunning, and he is certainly very strong. If you escort us, I will reward you. I request no service beyond that, and I recognize that you and Krampus are both free men."

Agios looked at Krampus. Caspar was offering them a purpose for at least the months of the journey. After that, maybe he and Krampus could find a place to settle far from haunting memories. "If our obligation ends once we arrive at your destination, we will accept," he said.

"You will be well compensated," Caspar assured him. "I know that my two friends will want to contribute, too. You will never have to face the dangers of harvesting frank-incense again."

It was more than Agios could have hoped for.

That night, as they sat near the fire, Gamos seemed troubled. "What did he tell you about the trip?"

"Not much," Agios admitted. "I don't care, though. We are going away from these lands, and that's all that matters to me."

Gamos stirred the embers of the campfire, the firelight sketching his craggy face in lines of yellow. "You'll be traveling into Roman territory—a dangerous journey."

"So?"

Gamos looked across the fire at him. "He's taking none of us soldiers as guards. You know the Romans?"

"By reputation only," Agios said. He added drily, "Mostly I've heard about their slave trade."

Krampus whimpered at the mention of the word "slave"—or maybe "Romans."

Gamos sighed. "Do you know what has been happening among the Romans?"

Agios shook his head. "That's nothing to me."

"You ought to know, though, before you go among them. You've heard of Julius Caesar, who died forty years ago or more?"

"A soldier, wasn't he? I have heard the name."

Gamos took a swig of wine. "Ruler of Rome. Enemies assassinated him. For years there was civil war, until his kinsman Octavian defeated the armies of Caesar's assassins. Octavian had himself crowned emperor of all Rome's possessions—he took the name Caesar Augustus, 'the honored Caesar.' You know of Augustus?"

Agios shrugged. "That name I have not heard."

"Well, he believes in military might," Gamos said, a note of admiration creeping into his voice. "He's a good leader of soldiers."

"What has this to do with me?" Agios asked.

Gamos took a few moments before answering. Then he held out his hand and made a fist as he said, "Augustus has tightened the Romans' grip in that part of the world. Rome is master of Syria, Palestine, and Egypt. You know the Romans' way of ruling?"

"They make conquered countries provinces of their empire," Agios said. "They set up governors and make Roman law the law of the land."

"Do you know much of their religion?"

Agios shook his head. "Gods and goddesses, like most

religions, but I don't know the names of the Roman ones. I've told you religion doesn't mean much to me."

The fire had burned low as the night waned, and in the faint, flickering light Gamos fell silent for a while. Then he said, "Like most peoples, the Romans worship many gods. The chief is Jove, who is said to rule the sky and all beneath it, and then come his brothers Neptune, who rules the sea, and Pluto, who is king of the dead. Many others. However, when the Romans seize control of a country, they let the people continue to worship their own gods. So in Egypt there are still temples to Ra, the sun god, and all the other Egyptian deities. All the Romans demand is that the locals recognize Roman gods, even with a token sacrifice."

Agios listened but had no comment other than a short grunt of understanding.

"Some locals, though, resist that. The Hebrews are one such group. Do you know of them?"

"I've met some," Agios said. "I've learned a little of their language. It is a dialect of Aramaic."

"Oh," Gamos said appreciatively. "That will be an advantage." Then he continued: "They believe in just one God.

And they believe their God—I don't know his name—commands that they worship no one else. They refuse even the token sacrifice the Romans demand. You see?"

"Not really," Agios replied.

Gamos lowered his voice: "Caspar and the others plan to go to the land of the Hebrews. It is not safe there. I have heard whispers of uprisings. Of revolt."

Agios was no soldier, but he did not recoil at the thought of war. If he had reason, he would gladly stand and fight, for the sorrow in his spirit was slowly hardening into something different altogether. Bitterness. Anger. It would feel good to go into battle.

Gamos sighed. "I wish Caspar would take six or eight of us guards with him. Promise me you'll look out for him, Agios. I have been in his service more years than I can reckon without a careful count."

"I'll do what I can," Agios said.

"That is all I ask."

"What will you do?"

"The rest of the caravan will travel on," Gamos told him. We are on our way to Khor Rori, the port city. We'll trade what we have and load the camels with goods to carry home. If the gods will it, we will meet Caspar again on the trade route, or failing that, back in his kingdom."

Agios did not reply. It was a troubled world. He wondered if he would ever feel at home in it again.

Gamos eventually fell asleep with his cloak pulled over his head, and Krampus was able to find rest, too. The bulky man snored and tossed fitfully, but Agios was grateful that he could sleep without fear or pain.

In the firelight, Krampus's ugly face lost its seeming fierceness. In sleep, the big man had an expression of sorrow. Agios wondered about his past, his sufferings. He suspected the simple man had known nothing besides mistreatment and the sting of the lash. It would take time to undo what had been done to him. Not for the first time, Agios wondered at the men who had abused him. It was exactly as he had suspected: Krampus was not a monster, but simply a man starved for kindness. He didn't look or act or talk like other men, but he had something gentle, something childlike in him. Agios had seen it the very first time he laid eyes on him.

Because he couldn't sleep, Agios pulled out his knife. He had pocketed two small pieces of wood earlier and he chose one now, a long, thin piece that would serve his purpose perfectly.

It took hours to carve, and the sun was just spilling gold across the horizon when he put the finishing touches on one of the wings. He had never seen a picture of one of these creatures, but Gamos had spoken of them, and now Agios had made his best effort at capturing its likeness. The dragon was a thing of beauty—his best effort yet—and he marveled at it for a moment. The sleek, scaly body curved sinuously, the tail coiled like a snake. That hadn't been the hard part. Agios had labored over the wings, spread wide and marvelous, and the tiny, pointed teeth in the open, roaring mouth. Agios smiled a little, then placed the beast on the ground next to Gamos. It would be the first thing he would see when he opened his eyes. It was the only way Agios could think to say good-bye.

Quietly, Agios woke Krampus. Pressing his finger to his lips, he helped the giant to his feet and they slipped away in the predawn light. The horses were saddled and ready, and so was Caspar. Without even uttering a greeting, Agios took the spear a servant offered him and slid a short sword into the leather strap across his back. Krampus would not mount.

"Let him go on foot," Agios said.

"He will slow us."

"If we try to gallop the whole way, we'll kill the horses."

"True," said Caspar. In the end, two on horseback and one jogging tirelessly along, they left the caravan and headed north as a dry wind stirred up clouds of dust.

Chapter 5

Caspar explained that the journey would take close to two weeks, and they would have to trade and hunt to survive along the way. Hunting was no problem—very little could evade Agios's spear—but he worried about the trading. Caspar had said that the surplus frankincense could be sold for food or for unexpected needs, new horseshoes or reins to replace worn-out ones—but Agios knew that frankincense would rouse suspicion and greed. It wouldn't be long before their reputation preceded them, and when that happened, they would likely find themselves in a perilous situation.

"All will be well," Caspar assured him. "We have the brute."

"His name is Krampus," Agios insisted. "Even with him, we are only three. We can be outnumbered and defeated."

Caspar thought for a moment. "I have an idea."

At the next village they traded for hot bowls of a rich lentil stew, several crusty loaves of barley bread, and some oddities that Caspar was very secretive about. First they secured six balls of yarn and a dozen small earthenware vessels. Then Caspar visited a seller of medicines and curious chemicals. That night, as they sat with their mats unrolled beside a low fire, Caspar unpacked bags and flasks of powders and mixed them until he tossed a pinch of it into the campfire. It flared like lightning, blinding, and sent a wave of heat that scorched Agios's face. An acrid boiling smoke remained. "Good," Caspar said. "An acid will make it take fire." He produced small flasks with corks, prepared them, and then wound skeins of wool around a bag full of the powders and one of the flasks. When he was finished, they each had two balls of wool that they tucked carefully inside their cloaks.

Caspar showed them how one loop of wool was left. "Pull the loop and it uncorks the flask inside. The acid mixes with the powder, and . . ." Caspar mimed an explosion with his hands.

Krampus twitched the loop on one of the two balls of wool he held.

"Not now," Agios told him quickly, putting a warning hand on the man's broad arm. "It's dangerous."

Krampus seemed to understand.

As the fire slowly burned to glowing coals, Caspar and Krampus gave in to sleep. But Agios couldn't find rest. Staring into the dying fire, he suddenly became aware that the land was bathed in light, nearly as bright as a full moon on the desert. Yet the moon was well past full, and in a different part of the sky. Agios got to his feet and saw that halfway to the zenith and off to the northwest a star shone, an unfamiliar one. Its brilliance astonished him.

Krampus muttered in his sleep and stirred slightly.

Staring at the star, Agios felt a stirring of memory almost as sharp as longing.

A light in the night. Darkness all around.

He had dreamed of this, dreamed of something even more valuable than frankincense. Something that he him-self lacked.

But as a brisk wind lifted the hem of his cloak, Agios turned from the star and its unusual light. It was part of the heavens, an unearthly fantasy of the sort that Philos used to believe in. His son had wished on stars. But Agios knew that was foolishness. The star was nothing but far-off light and impossible yearning: a dream.

In spite of the harsh, unforgiving landscape, they journeyed as quickly as they could toward the city of Megisthes, where Melchior ruled, prodded forward by Caspar's desire to join his friends and their shared anxiety about the safety of the trade route. They found themselves in a dry land with high sandstone cliffs. The rock face was honeycombed with caves—the dwelling places of lepers and outcasts, Caspar told him.

The day grew unbearably hot and Caspar called for a midday break. They watered the stallions in a nearby stream and then tethered them in the shade of a small stand of trees. Caspar took out his bedroll and in minutes dropped into a doze, apparently confident that his guards would let nothing escape their watchful gaze. But Krampus's eyes were fixed on the caves—not the road.

Agios watched his charge. He suspected that Krampus was much younger than he had originally supposed—

maybe as young as his mid-teens. But there was no way to know for sure. He was slowly learning to speak, gaining in confidence daily. He usually talked, though, only of immediate needs, food or drink or the need to relieve himself. Never of the past. Perhaps he did not even comprehend time as other men did.

Crouching down beside him, Agios motioned to the hills and the dwellings that Krampus seemed so fixated on. "Where do you come from?" he asked.

No answer but a grunt.

Agios tried in the handful of other languages he knew. Krampus did not respond at all, until Agios spoke Latin: "Where do you come from?"

Krampus growled and shook his head. He mimed pulling at an oar.

"Yes, I heard you were a galley slave. Before that, though? Where did you live? Who were your father and mother?"

Krampus stared at Agios for a moment, and then he turned fully away, giving Agios his back. It was a childish move, a clear indication that he didn't want to talk and, even more likely, didn't want to remember. Agios could understand. He clapped a hand on Krampus's shoulder for just a moment, and then walked away to give him privacy. A measure of peace. Even from several strides away, Agios could hear the muffled, gargling sound that came from deep inside Krampus's throat. It was the sound of his weeping.

At least I know he understands Latin. Perhaps, Agios thought, he should use that tongue to speak with Krampus. He might be quicker to talk in his native language.

The three men saw their destination a day before they reached it. Megisthes was a fortified city in the mountains, a place of domes and spires. It ran along a ridge and commanded valleys on three sides, in morning light a shining, rose-colored metropolis carved in stone. Farms lush with produce nearly ready for harvest crowded the valleys. They were an anomaly in the barren mountains, but Megisthes seemed perched on a vast oasis.

They camped outside the city and the next morning Caspar, Agios, and Krampus took a long, winding road across the plain and up to the broad summit of the ridge, where guards allowed them to pass through a gate and into the outer courtyards of Megisthes. Agios saw that the streets, though narrow, were carefully paved with precisely cut pale sandstone. The houses and buildings were of pinkish granite, and though crowded, the place seemed well ordered, the people happy. They appeared to recognize Caspar, but they shot curious glances at Agios and Krampus. No one spoke to them as an armed man led the three to the inner city and to the gates of an enormous palace.

Word had been sent ahead and a second guard met them at the inner gate and then led Caspar, Agios, and Krampus into a collection of airy, comfortable rooms. They found Melchior in his library, surrounded by a hundred or more scrolls. He rose from his seat at a table: a tall, dark-haired man with a flowing black beard and brown eyes that had the faraway gaze of a scholar.

He was taller than Agios by a few finger-breadths, though not as muscular. He wore a gray knee-length tunic, the garment belted at the waist, and Greek sandals. His expression seemed open and honest and his features had the mark of intelligence.

"Caspar!" he called, crossing the room to embrace his old friend. "It's good to see you. The time of the prophecy is near."

The two men embraced, and then Caspar turned to introduce Melchior to Agios. As a hired guard and nothing more, Agios hadn't expected to be allowed into Melchior's home, much less treated as a man of any significance. But Caspar seemed full of surprises.

Agios bowed slightly and then gestured at Krampus. Ill at ease as he generally was beneath a roof, Krampus shambled a step toward him. "This is Krampus. He's my friend and a strong fighter. He will help us defend ourselves."

Krampus looked at Agios for direction. Agios bent his head, and Krampus imitated him.

Without reacting to either Krampus's size or his ugliness, Melchior said, "You are welcome, too. I hope we will have no need of violence, but I am grateful for your strength."

Krampus grinned, obviously pleased, at least at Melchior's tone. Agios doubted that he understood any of the words.

Caspar told Melchior, "I have explained that the trip may be difficult. We will be few in number, and we will be carrying valuable things. I don't wish to take a guard of any size—our mission is not a political one, and the less warlike we seem, the easier it will be to pass borders. Are you in agreement, Melchior?"

"Certainly, if these two men are willing to fight."

Agios nodded but held his tongue.

Melchior looked at him silently and then asked, "What gods do you worship, Agios?"

"None," Agios confessed.

Looking surprised, Melchior asked, "None at all? Are you a complete unbeliever?"

Agios told him, "My people have no gods, though we believe that everything has a spirit of its own. But as for worship, no, I have no god to pray to. If I have faith in anything, sir, it's in spirit and in life. I can't believe in gods. It's hard enough for me to believe in people."

Caspar smiled. "Though our friend is not a man without *any* beliefs, or without any sense of spirit."

"I wonder more than believe," Agios corrected.

Melchior asked, "But how do you feel if others believe?"

With a shrug, Agios said, "So long as it harms no one, let each believe as he wishes."

"Well, well," Melchior said, his voice thoughtful. "Perhaps you may find more to believe in by and by." He rang a bell, and a servant came to the library doorway.

"These men are tired after a long ride," Melchior told him. "See that they have baths and fresh clothing and a good meal."

Agios explained Krampus's special needs—the big

man would never sleep inside a building or tent, but insisted on being in the open, or at least in a place where he could see the sky—and the servants found a room for Agios with a balcony outside. Krampus indicated that he would be content to sleep there, out in the air. They bathed and donned fresh clothing provided by Melchior, and later they ate together. The two scholars dined elsewhere. Krampus obviously relished the food—roast peafowl and goat's meat—and when they had finished, he spread his arms, as if to take in the entire place, perhaps the entire kingdom. "Good," he said. For him it was quite a speech.

That night as Agios readied himself for bed, a servant came to the room. "Melchior commands your presence," the servant said. Agios checked on Krampus, who had fallen into a sound sleep, and he followed the servant to a tower built into a corner of the city wall—a tower far too tall to be a defensive post.

The servant said, "He awaits you at the top."

A spiral stairway of many hundred steps led up and up. Agios climbed steadily, though his thighs began to ache just past the midway point. The stair ended on a flat, roofless platform. Agios stepped out into the night. A sky like black

velvet stretched overhead, sprinkled with stars looking unusually bright, for the moon had not risen.

"Come here," Melchior said. He was a silhouette in the
darkness.

Agios felt the fresh breeze of the mountains. In the faint
starlight he could tell only that Melchior stood alone. With
some caution Agios walked across the platform to stand
near him.

"Caspar just left me. He suggested I show you a few
things. This way is north," Melchior said, taking Agios's
upper arm and turning him so he looked out over the low
parapet. "Do you know the stars?"

"I know some have names for them," Agios said. "The
Babylonians call one Ishtar. My own people didn't name
the stars, but I can tell my way from them." He looked up.
"There is the North Star, for example. It is always in the
night sky and shows a true direction."

"Look straight ahead, and to the west, and a third of the
way up from the horizon. Do you see that star, the bright-
est one?"

He couldn't have missed it: a star as bright as the Morning Star or Evening Star, nearly as bright as a beacon,
brighter than the last time he had caught sight of it. It flared

and seemed to shoot brilliant beams of light. "I see it, sir. I noticed it in the desert some days ago."

"It is a new star," Melchior said, his voice taut with an underlying excitement. "It is not a wandering star, of the kind the Greeks call *planeta*. I don't think it is a fixed star, at least not one of the ordinary kind, for the whole dome of the sky slowly rotates through the year, turning around the axis of the North Star, but for the ten months since that one appeared, it has been in the very same place, growing steadily brighter. The planets roam, the fixed stars rotate but keep their patterns—but that star alone is faithful to its place in the heavens."

Agios didn't know what to say. He grunted thoughtfully.

"It is something new," Melchior said. "It's an omen."

Omens. They crammed the world full, if you listened to all the priests of all the religions. A crow flying overhead was an omen, or an oddly shaped fruit, or the cry of a wolf, or an earthquake or a storm, or drought or flood, wind or calm. *Omens everywhere, and most of them evil*, Agios thought.

As though reading his mind, Melchior said, "This one means something good, Agios. Something wonderful. I've read about it in the old scrolls and have discussed it with wise men. My friends Caspar and Balthasar have seen it, too. Balthasar is on his way and will be here in the next few days. We must prepare. If the prophecies are true, if this is the sign in the heavens I've been looking for, that star will grow steadily brighter. When it is as bright as the full moon, we must leave. That may be in a few days or in a few weeks—there's no telling. When the time comes, we must begin our search."

"And what do you hope to find, sir?"

"Someone to whom Balthasar, Caspar, and I must bow," Melchior said.

Agios tried to peer through the darkness but he couldn't quite make out Melchior's features. "Mithridates?" he asked, naming the man he recalled as ruler of the entire Parthian Empire.

"Mithridates died years ago," Melchior said. "Phraates holds the throne now—but I don't mean him, either."

"Then who?" Agios asked.

Melchior took a deep breath. When he spoke again, his voice was low and full of awe: "I mean the hope of the world, the one whose coming is foretold in prophecy. I mean a King of Kings."

It was the second time Agios had heard the term. This time it made him shiver.

Chapter 6

B althasar arrived the following day. He was from the far southern desert country, a swarthy, heavyset man of great vigor. He spoke the common language, Aramaic, with a pronounced accent and a booming voice. As soon as he met the others, the three prepared for the journey. Agios and Krampus stayed out of the way, but after nightfall Melchior invited Agios once again to the observation tower. Krampus remained below, on solid ground.

Agios followed the three scholar-kings up the stair. When they arrived on the platform, Balthasar cried out in wonder. "This is the clearest I've ever seen it," he said. "It is a glory in the heavens."

"Is it as bright as the full moon?" Melchior asked.

Balthasar gazed. "Very nearly, I think. Much brighter than it was only two nights ago."

"Then we leave tomorrow."

"I agree," Balthasar said.

Caspar asked, "Have we all our gifts?"

Melchior said, "I have thought long about the question, and as my gift I bring gold, the purest that I could find, as is proper for a gift to a great king."

Balthasar murmured in reply, "That is well done. There will be need of gold, whoever his family might be. I bring a cask of myrrh. It's very costly. In my country people burn it as an offering to the gods. It is said to have a calming effect on a troubled spirit. It is, I think, fit as a gift to a great healer of souls."

"And I bring frankincense, a resin more costly than gold." Caspar said. "If the family is in need, they can trade it for whatever they desire. No merchant would refuse even a fly's weight of it."

In the silver light of the star, Balthasar looked impressed. "I know of it. It's surpassingly rare. In my land, doctors prescribe it as a medicine for the relief of pain."

Caspar, whose face was normally expressive of enjoyment, nodded and looked solemn. "There will be much pain in his life, as there is in the life of every great man," he said. "And he will take upon himself the pain of the world. Frankincense cannot ease that, but perhaps it may hearten him to know that there is an end to every pain, and that those who care will offer what relief they may."

Balthasar was silent before asking, "With all these riches, do we travel with a strong guard?"

Caspar said, "With only two men. With Agios here and with the giant Krampus."

"Giant?"

"That's an exaggeration," Melchior said. "But he is taller than most, and very strong. You have not seen him yet. Don't let his looks startle you. He's loyal to Agios, and I think with him we need no stronger guard."

"May it be so," Balthasar said.

Melchior said, "I'll have my men prepare our animals. Let us get what sleep we can. We will set off in the afternoon and will travel mostly by night, for the star will be our guide. Agios, tell Krampus."

"I will," Agios said. "He will need no camel or horse, though. He prefers to walk."

"That will slow us."

"No," Agios said. "He is untiring."

"Very well."

And with that they all separated. Agios checked on Krampus: He slept soundly, out on the terrace. He had turned and the light of the new star fell full in his face, softening his grotesque features, making him look at peace and—well, not exactly normal, but certainly no monster. What had warped and twisted him, beyond Roman cruelty? Agios did not know, but reflected that the deformity had not reached Krampus's heart. For that he was grateful.

The journey was nothing like those Agios had experienced before. The caravan was slow and lumbering, and the long ride on horseback to Megisthes was exhausting. Now Caspar, Balthasar, and Melchior rode on camels, and four more camels bore the loads of their provisions and gifts. Sturdy mules carried tents and awnings. Agios rode the same horse he had left the caravan with, a fine stallion that kept pace with the camels even on trackless, rocky expanses. Krampus walked beside Agios, alert, head back, always sniffing the air.

The route took them across a desert landscape called Nafud: expanses of tawny-red sand broken by outcrops of wind-eroded red rock, with no shade, no trees, no plant life at all except for tough, low-growing spindly brush, allium and crucifer, and scorpion senna and germander.

The group traveled in the late afternoons and well into the night, sometimes past sunrise. As the sun climbed to the zenith, its heat became like a weight on their shoulders, and as the air danced and shimmered, the land looked no more solid than the sea. In the ovenlike heat they spread awnings and rested in the meager shade. At these times Caspar himself continued to teach Agios how to read, and soon Melchior and Balthasar also began to offer instruction. "You have a real gift for languages," Melchior once told him admiringly. When they grew tired of teaching and reading, they all snatched what sleep they could.

One night as they threaded their way along the winding floor of a dry wadi, Krampus suddenly grunted. "What is it?" Agios asked.

"Someone," Krampus muttered, and in the pale light filtering down from the starry sky Agios saw him gesture.

"Let me ride ahead," Agios said to Caspar. "Wait until I know it's safe."

He urged his mount forward, peering into the darkness. A deeper shadow moved toward him. "What do you have worth taking?" asked a harsh voice.

"Nothing," Agios said. "And if you try to take anything, you'll regret it."

He felt the press of a spear against his back. A second bandit, who had waited still and unseen in the darkness.

"I think not," the first said.

Agios sighed and reached to his belt. "All I have are these," he said, taking out a ball of wool.

The first bandit came close enough to snatch it from his grasp. "Foolishness!"

"It's what the wool is wrapped around that is valuable," Agios said. He saw the man fumble with the wound skein. "I wouldn't unwrap it," he said, and averted his eyes.

The flash of brilliant fire came, spooking the bandit's horse and making the man shriek. Agios spun, grabbed the second robber's spear, and yanked.

The first man rolled on the ground, moaning, his robes smoldering with red writhing sparks. The second one tried to draw a sword—but Krampus had run up and grasped his arm.

No other robbers appeared. The travelers caught up

with them. Caspar saw to it that both men had been disarmed. The one who had been burned wept and said, "I'm blind!"

"Your eyes may heal in time," Caspar said. "You and your friend will have to walk for help. We'll leave you enough water for one day."

"Not enough!" the man said, his voice jagged with fear.

"I told you not to unwrap it," Agios said. The scholars rode on, leading the robbers' two horses, leaving the bandits behind in the dark. Miles later, at dawn, Caspar let the horses go. "Maybe they'll find their way back to their riders," he said. "I do not like to leave the men with no hope of living."

Agios began to doubt they themselves would survive the journey, but then one morning they came within sight of a green spot in the sand, an oasis where a spring bubbled into a round pool perhaps fifteen cubits across. Four goatherds had built a stone shelter there and stared in wonder as the five men and their animals staggered in from the desert.

The men and animals drank. Agios had not realized how thirsty he had been. He swallowed and swallowed, and all at once his whole body began to sweat. Krampus drank even more deeply, his throat bobbing as he gulped.

They bought goat's flesh from the herdsmen and cooked it over a fire of dried dung. Agios was sure it was the most delicious thing he had ever tasted.

That night, Melchior seemed restless. Agios found him past midnight, a little way from their camp, on top of a stony outcrop. He stood gazing at the sky as though he could not tear himself away from the sight of the star.

In the dry desert air it flared brighter than ever. "It is even more brilliant than the full moon," Melchior murmured as Agios joined him. "Look, I can read by its light." He held up a thin scroll and turned to let the star's illumination fall on the parchment.

In his own language, Melchior read aloud, "I shall see him, but not now: I shall behold him, but not nigh: there shall come a Star out of Jacob, and a Scepter shall rise out of Israel." He translated.

"Star of Jacob? I don't understand," Agios said. "Does it mean that star?"

"Perhaps," Melchior said softly. "These are the words of Balaam, a man of the old time. Some say he was a magician, others a prophet." He sighed. "I've long searched for the star, through weary nights of standing on the tower platform there in the east and gazing to the west. A good way westward from my kingdom is the land of the Israelites. I think this must be the star I've waited for so long."

"You are very eager to follow it."

"And afraid," Melchior said.

"What? What is there to fear?"

"A great change is coming, Agios. In change there is always fear."

Always afterward, Agios remembered that leg of their journey, taken at night across a desert visible in the light of the moon and of the star. It seemed like a dream, even while he lived it. It was as though every man and woman and child, every animal but the ones they rode, had died and emptied the earth of life.

Balthasar knew ways that none of the others did. He led them into a ravine. At the bottom a shallow stream ran, nowhere more than ankle-deep, but it flowed northwest. Now they traveled by daylight, for the narrow gorge shielded them from the sun except for a few hours on either side of noon.

The water was bitter and faintly salty, but it could be drunk, and they followed the stream until it emptied into a larger river. They began to run into tiny villages, mere temporary gatherings of herdsmen and hunters. The people stared at the strangers—and gasped at the sight of

Krampus, whose smile always looked more like a threatening scowl. Finally the travelers came to a land more forgiving—still an arid country, but one where enough water fell from the sky or flowed through the streams to support farms and small towns.

Passing through ranges of low, dust-colored hills, they journeyed through a countryside where palm trees grew, where dates and other fruits would be abundant in season. They did not linger, but hurried on their way.

One morning an expanse of gleaming water appeared ahead, not a river but a great lake or sea. "It is salty," Balthasar told them. "Deadly to drink, saltier than the great Mediterranean. They call it the Dead Sea. We will skirt the northern edge, and we will be in Judea. Jerusalem should be only a few days' travel now. Herod is king there, the second Herod, son of the man who died some years ago. He rules the land of Judea."

"Under the Romans," Melchior said.

"Yes, the Romans are his masters," Balthasar agreed. "However, I have heard he is a proud man, so we will not mention that to him. In his court we may find wise men who can counsel us. After all, we don't yet know just where we will find the new king."

Roman soldiers stopped them often, always making Krampus restless and anxious. Melchior had letters of passage, and after some delay, an occasional bribe, and some bureaucratic grumbling, the soldiers always allowed the party to go on. They headed across salt pans and waste places, now and then coming to settlements or seeing shepherds tending their flocks.

Finally they arrived in the city, not the largest Agios had ever seen, but one teeming with life. That afternoon they found a place to stay at an inn with spacious stables for the animals. The precious gifts they stored in one room, and Krampus settled by the one door leading into it. On a wax tablet Melchior wrote an appeal for an audience with Herod, and Agios found a Roman soldier, a centurion, who for a small silver piece was willing to take the letter to the palace. "Don't expect a quick answer, though," the man warned Agios. "The king has a thousand things on his mind."

And so they waited for three days before a summons came: Herod would see Melchior, Caspar, and Balthasar, but they must come alone and unarmed.

Melchior asked if they might bring their translator. Agios glanced quickly at Melchior. Is that what the scholars were calling him now? Their translator? Agios was no such thing, even though he had gained a passable command of a handful of languages. The soldier didn't know if Agios would be allowed to enter, but told him to come along. If the king refused, he would have to wait at the palace gate, that was all.

Agios had spent most of his time sitting next to Krampus and idly carving. He told Krampus to stay on guard, promising to return soon. "Soon?" the big man asked anxiously.

"Don't worry," Agios told him. "Stay here. No one will bother you."

Krampus dropped his gaze. "Roman soldiers," he muttered. "Whips. Chains."

It's the most he's ever spoken all at once, Agios thought, *and the words are fear and bitterness*. He asked softly, "Do you trust me?"

Krampus nodded.

"Then do as I ask, my friend. I will return."

"Friend," Krampus said in a voice that broke Agios's heart. He went to his pack and brought back a handful of his carvings. Krampus smiled at last, and Agios left him, taking with him a bag of the little figures he had made on the long journey.

As they walked through the teeming streets, every time he saw a young boy or girl, Agios would reach into the bag and leave the gift so the child could easily find it. On a low fence, perched on the edge of a basket, tossed in the path. Some were representations of things he had seen in the desert: a scorpion, a lizard, a kind of hawk-billed bird. Others were more familiar animals: camels, lambs, even dogs and cats. Though small, the carvings were wonderfully detailed.

Often before Agios had gone three steps the children discovered the gifts with delight. Agios pretended that he didn't notice.

Melchior turned and said, "Agios, hurry! You're falling behind."

"Coming," Agios said, and he quickened his pace.

Caspar quietly said, "You stand apart from mankind, but I think your heart softens toward children."

Agios said gruffly, "I once had a son." His tone was so rough that none of the men asked anything more.

They ran into more delay at the palace gate as the request to bring their translator with them was sent in to Herod. Agios imagined the process: The gate captain reported to his commander. The commander went to the guardsman in charge of the inner gate. That guardsman went to the commander of the king's personal guard. That man asked the king's advisor. The advisor asked the king. The king pondered and gave his answer, and then the whole thing had to be repeated in reverse. When men ruled over men, time was wasted and misspent.

After perhaps an hour the answer came: Agios might enter with the others.

A guard led them through corridors lined with pillars and hung with tapestries. In an inner sanctum lighted by a skylight, Herod sat upon a throne raised on a dais. It looked like gold, but Agios thought it was probably made of gilded wood. He had ordered three seats, low, to be placed before the throne, and on these he invited his royal visitors to sit. Agios, being a commoner, stood behind Melchior.

While each of the scholars briefly introduced himself, Agios studied Herod's features. He was a gaunt man, not old—surely not much more than thirty—but high-cheeked and with deep-set eyes that added at least a decade to his appearance. His hair was short and brushed forward in the Roman fashion. When the others had all spoken their greetings and introductions, Herod said quietly, "Welcome to you, travelers. I am Herod, tetrarch of Judea. Why have you come, men of the East?"

Melchior became the spokesman: "Your Majesty, we are

men who study prophecy and the stars. Our researches have shown that a great event is to take place in your kingdom—may already have taken place, in fact. We have come from far away to witness a moment that will change the world."

"And what is that?" Herod asked. He had a smooth voice, low and confident.

"My lord," Melchior said, "a great king is to be born in Judea. One day he will be known as King of Kings, ruler of all good men. We have come to witness his coming, and we wish to worship him."

Herod stared. "Men are not to be worshipped," he said sharply, then caught himself, and his voice took on its oily smoothness again: "Unless, of course, they're great men, like Julius Caesar, the father of the great emperor of Rome."

Melchior continued: "Sire, the prophecies tell us that this child will become greater than any king or emperor the world has ever known. He will lift men's spirits and will save their souls. That is why we come to worship him."

Herod stroked his chin with long, twitching fingers. "Indeed? Tell me how you know these things."

Agios understood most of the words but could make little of the discussion that followed. Melchior spoke of ancient writings, read some of them aloud to Herod, then talked of signs and wonders he and the others had witnessed. He mentioned the progression of the stars in the heavens through the year, told of how the planets wandered and changed position from night to night, and spoke of the extraordinary star that did not follow any rules. Herod listened attentively.

When Melchior fell silent, Herod asked, "Do you know where to find this young king?"

Melchior admitted, "No, sire. Because of the prophecies we've read, we know he is to spring from Galilee, and that is all."

"Oh, Galilee." Herod sounded amused. "It's a big enough place to make your search difficult. And it may disappoint you. Do you know that Galilee is where many pretenders have sprung up, many so-called magicians and prophets? You will not find a true king in Galilee."

Caspar, who could not follow the conversation easily, looked to Agios, who bent toward him and quietly explained what he had understood. Caspar said, "Tell the king that we have seen evidence. Speak of the star."

Agios asked for permission to speak, and when Herod granted it, he translated Caspar's words: "In the East we have seen his star. It is a wondrous sign, one that no human could imitate or cause to appear. It is surely the work of God. That is why we have come to worship the King of Kings."

"The star again?" Herod asked. He summoned one of his servants and had a whispered talk with him. While the travelers waited uneasily, Herod called in a white-bearded elderly man and murmured questions that the old man answered. At length Herod waved him away.

Then he said, "I have heard something of a new star, a strange star, from this man, one of my many scholars. I will consult them. You may have a meal and wait while I confer with them. I don't wish you to leave the palace yet, for this news interests me. My servants will attend you while I speak to my astrologers."

Two servants ushered them into a banquet hall far too large for four men, and serving girls brought them dishes of honey, loaves of bread, figs, olives, dates, and pomegranates. They poured a strong red wine into golden cups. Agios, who usually ate only with Krampus, stood near the doorway, but Melchior told him to sit with the scholars and join in the feast. He ate, but he drank no wine.

"You don't like it?" Balthasar asked, holding up his cup.

"Wine makes me foolish," Agios said. "Unless I mingle it with a great deal of water, I prefer not to drink it."

One of the serving girls brought him a pitcher of water, and then he did drink, splashing only a taste of the wine into the cup. "This is too fine a vessel for a hunter," he murmured, holding up the cup.

"You have become more than a hunter," Melchior told him.

"Have I?" Agios asked.

They finished the meal, then waited. Caspar paced the floor, shaking his head with impatience. "The kings in these over-civilized parts of the world take too long in making up their minds," he said. "In the desert, we see a need and we move!"

At last in the midafternoon a guard summoned them back into the presence of Herod. The king had changed his robes and now wore one of splendid purple, a color reserved only for the highest royalty. He gestured them back to their seats and said, "I have heard all about the new star now. My scholars tell me it is possibly an omen, though they admit they can't interpret its meaning, as you seem to think you have done. When did you first notice it, now, I wonder?"

"The first time for me," Melchior said, "was when the star was so faint and dim that anyone else would easily have overlooked it. That was nearly a year ago." He named the exact date, and Herod called in one of his own scholars to work out how Melchior's calendar correlated with the Roman one. For some reason, the exact timing of the star's appearance seemed very important to him.

"Then if your belief is true," Herod said, "if the star appeared, say, at the time the new king was born, then he must be close to a year old."

Melchior spread his hands. "Perhaps. Or perhaps the star appeared at his conception, and maybe he is newly born— our knowledge doesn't extend that far. We will know only when we seek him and find him."

"But you believe he is a child, an infant."

"So we believe," Melchior agreed.

Herod nodded. "Then go to Galilee," he said. "Find your King of Kings. I give you this commandment, though: when you find the child, return here to my palace and tell me exactly where he is." When the three visitors did not immediately respond, Herod smiled and said in his smoothest voice, "I wish to worship him, too."

"Very well," Melchior replied.

By the time they left the palace night was coming on. "We will find him," Melchior said, and Agios didn't know if he was talking to himself or to his friends. "Even if it should take years. We will begin tomorrow—"

But Caspar had stopped in his tracks. "Come," he said urgently. "Let's find an open place." Without explanation, he led them through the streets and finally out into a plaza or square. That was not enough. At the inn, he bargained with the innkeeper, who didn't understand what he asked for, but who finally provided a ladder, of all things. They used it to climb to the flat roof of the stables. "Look," Caspar said, pointing upward.

Agios frowned. The western sky showed a bright cluster of stars—but not the great star. "It's gone!" he said.

"No," Caspar said, half turning toward the south. "It has moved."

They gasped. The familiar star, more brilliant than ever, reigned in the southeast. It shot glorious rays of light, beams in all the colors of a rainbow.

"What does this mean?" Balthasar asked.

Melchior spoke, calmly enough, but with an edge of excitement in his voice: "It means that we will leave Jerusalem tonight. It means that we must follow the star."

Chapter 7

During daylight hours, the broad plaza outside the Bethlehem Gate bustled and buzzed as farmers hauled in produce to sell: lentils, beans, onions, apples, figs, and dates, and many other fruits of the earth, making the air fragrant. Shepherds and goatherds sold bleating lambs and kids. Camels and donkeys and horses brought burdens in from distant lands for trade, and their dung added its smell to the air.

Even at night some merchants lingered there, along with torchlit booths of moneychangers who would, for a fee, exchange the currency of India for that of Rome, or Egyptian money for Persian. Agios led the way through the late crowds, shrugging off the merchants who wished to make one last sale, and once a roaring Krampus frightened away a bold, thieving wench who tried to steal Melchior's money pouch from his belt.

"How far to Galilee?" Balthasar asked.

Agios didn't know, but he spoke to some of the travelers who had come by camel until he found one who did. He told Balthasar, Caspar, and Melchior, "It's to the north, they say, many leagues away. If we go there, we turn our backs on the star."

"We will follow the star," Melchior said firmly. "The king springs from Galilee, but he might not be born there. We will go toward the star, traveling by night."

Caspar grunted in a discontented way.

"What's wrong, my friend?" Melchior asked him.

The desert scholar sounded troubled: "I don't trust Herod. He's . . . I can't say exactly. Too smooth. He's like a small mound of glittering sand, bright in the moonlight, under which lies a coiled viper."

The others were silent, but Agios agreed with Caspar. Herod's casual exercise of power hadn't been cruel, exactly, but it had been self-satisfied, as though he alone deserved to give orders and be obeyed. Caspar said, "Let's find the child and then we'll worry about Herod and his commands."

The others agreed. Agios spoke to more of the travelers in the plaza. The Romans said little, dismissing him as if he were a beggar. One old man, though, spoke of a census that had taken place over the past year. "Everyone had to go to the home of his forefathers to be registered," he said.

Melchior reflected, "Then our king's family may have come south from Galilee for the census."

"I trust the star," Balthasar said, and Caspar agreed.

All that night they took a tortuous path winding through a mountainous landscape. Toward dawn a thin layer of cloud crept in, hiding all stars but theirs. Its glow shone through, steady and sure.

Even when dawn came the three scholars and their two guards did not stop. They continued on a road that led between dry, dusty hills. In the forenoon they came to a wayside inn and paused to rest. "Where are we?" Agios asked the innkeeper. He told him, and Agios passed the news along to the others: "Not far to the south is a place where a holy woman named Rachel is buried. Beyond that is a town called Bethlehem. Then farther on—"

Caspar smiled and said, "Bethlehem! 'You, O Bethlehem, though little among the thousands of Judah, out of thee shall come forth unto me he who is to rule in Israel!'"

When Agios stared at him blankly, Caspar explained, "It is an ancient prophecy."

"Could it be so near?" Melchior asked.

Balthasar put a hand on his shoulder. In a voice trembling with emotion, he said, "We must wait until nightfall. Surely the star will lead us. If he is in Bethlehem, we will see him this night."

The three men embraced and wept. They did not notice when Agios and Krampus left to put away the camels and donkeys in the inn stables. As they fed and watered the animals, Agios felt troubled. It had been nearly a year since Philos had died. In some ways it felt like a lifetime ago, a time that belonged to another man. But the wound was still fresh and bleeding. Just the thought of new life, of a child so pure and full of potential, filled Agios with a sort of longing dread. Leaving his carvings for the children of Jerusalem was one thing, but Agios was not sure he could face an infant, much less a newborn king, an extraordinary child.

He did not go back into the inn, but in an unused stable he found a pile of sweet-smelling straw and lay on it, trying to get a little rest. Krampus sat close by, facing the open doorway, his back against a shaded wall and his bent, long arms wrapped around his knees. People passing the stables sometimes pointed at him and muttered, but with Agios there none of them taunted Krampus, and the ugly man fell into a doze. For Agios, sleep did not come. He had caught the excitement of the three wise kings, perhaps, or maybe he simply dreaded dreams of Philos.

None of the people who came into the stables spoke to him or bothered him. The time crept slowly by, and the heat grew. Agios thought of the high mountains where he had been born and raised, where he had married and fathered a child, of how desolate they could be in winter, how fresh and green in the spring. His heart ached, and he did not quite know why.

Late in the afternoon he finally drowsed. Then, suddenly, he woke all at once, fully aware, not slowly rising from sleep. His old hunting instincts kept him from moving. He heard breathing and cracked an eyelid.

Krampus was on his left, still sitting drawn up against the wall, now snoring gently. On Agios's right, not far from him, someone sat on his haunches, a man poorly dressed in a frayed woolen robe. He had a mop of black curly hair and he stared at Agios with brown, watchful eyes. As Agios raised himself up, the young fellow held up both hands as if in apology. "I did not mean to alarm you. I'm not a thief."

Agios rubbed a hand over his face. "I'm not alarmed."

The man—just a boy, really, in his late teens—blinked in surprise at hearing his own language spoken by a foreign-looking stranger. In nearly a whisper, maybe to avoid disturbing Krampus, he asked seriously, "Do you and your friends seek the—" He spoke a word that Agios had never heard before, one whispered so softly and reverently that he did not quite catch it.

"I don't understand that word," he said, rising up to sit on the straw. Despite the young man's assurances, Agios remained wary of him.

Slowly the young fellow said, "Messiah." He strung the word out a syllable at a time, but even though he struggled just to speak it clearly, his voice still held admiration, respect, maybe even awe.

"Messiah," Agios repeated after him. "What does it mean?"

With a shy smile, the stranger said, "I'm only a shepherd. I don't know how to teach words to a stranger. But Messiah, it is"—he waved his hands as though trying to catch a meaning in midair—"the promised one. A savior. The one who . . . rescues us from evil."

Agios said, "My friends have come many weary leagues to find the King of Kings."

The young shepherd's face nearly lit up with confidence and joy. "Ah. They seek the Messiah, then. Tell them Bethlehem. They must look in Bethlehem."

Agios could not help smiling at this ignorant boy's cheerful confidence. Had this shepherd solved the riddle that three great scholars still puzzled over? Unlikely. But Agios said in a friendly tone, "You sound very certain."

The young man paused for so long that Agios thought he would not speak again, but then he said softly, "I *am* certain." Agios felt something strange—the hair on his neck prickled, as it had done often enough when an elusive quarry was within sight. His heart felt strangely light. He caught his breath as the young man continued slowly, "I have seen him, the Messiah, the King of Kings. My friends and I have all seen him."

For some reason Agios's voice came hoarse: "Tell me." He spoke more loudly than he had meant to do, and Krampus murmured and stirred.

The shepherd gasped as Krampus looked up, revealing his misshapen features. Krampus gazed from the shepherd to Agios and back and made an inquiring rumble in his throat.

"It's all right, Krampus," Agios told him. "This man has a story that I'm interested in hearing."

The shepherd looked away, his face red. "You would never believe me."

"Tell us anyway," Agios said gently, in the same voice he had sometimes used to urge Philos to try something difficult. "We won't laugh at you."

Still not looking at Agios or Krampus directly, the shepherd boy took a deep breath. "It began," he said, "on a dark night. My friends and I were almost asleep, with two awake, watching over the sheep, the rest of us lying on our blankets under the sky."

He glanced back at Agios, who said, "I'm listening. Go on."

With a nod, the young man continued: "The older shepherds talked of this and that, the way they always do, about the price of wool, and complained about the Roman taxes, talked of the crowds of people registering for the Roman census. And then . . ."

His voice trailed off, and his face took on a yearning look, as if he had something tremendous to say but could not find suitable words. Agios waited him out, and at last the young shepherd said, "There appeared a man among us. He . . . he shone like the light of the stars. I can't describe him. He had a glow about him. I know it sounds crazy."

When he didn't speak for long moments, Agios asked, "A vision?"

"If it was some dream or vision, it was a very strange one, because we all shared it. Those of us who had been lying on our blankets leaped up. We were all afraid. The glowing man who had simply appeared among us . . . the *malakh*, you understand?"

"The messenger?" Agios asked. That was what the Aramaic term commonly meant, but an ordinary messenger would not cause such confusion, such reluctance, even in an uneducated shepherd boy.

"I have no tongue to speak!" the shepherd wailed. "The Greeks say *angelos*—angel, a messenger, yes, but from God!" Now, as though a dam had broken, his words gushed out: "The angel spoke to us and told us not to fear. Calm flowed from his voice like honey, sweet to our souls, and we lost our terror. We all fell to our knees on the grass. And then he told us a child was born in Bethlehem, a savior, the Christ whose birth was foretold long ago."

His voice caught, and he began to weep, tears pouring down his cheeks. For a time he could not speak, but shook his head as though pleading for breath enough to tell his story. Yet his expression was exalted.

With a catch in his words, he finally continued: "And—and then—oh, then, in the sky—oh, how can I tell you? We saw there, among the stars, a hundred, a thousand angels, singing of peace and of a king!"

Krampus whimpered, a strange sound, like a child seeing something that awed and fascinated him. Agios shushed him and said, "Go on, lad."

The shepherd strove to control himself and finally, humbly, he nearly whispered, "And so we all, oldest to youngest, went into town and found the child in a manger, for his family could find no room. We, the shepherds, the least of men, were the first to see the child and to worship him. We returned to our fields. Not a sheep had strayed. The lambs slept as though protected by God himself." His face shone again. "And we had seen the King of Kings."

Absurd, some would have said. A dream, or an outright lie. Agios, though, felt a strange assurance that every word the young man had said was true. "You have to tell the others."

And so Melchior, Caspar, and Balthasar heard the shepherd's story, told in detail to the very placement of the animals around the manger. None of them laughed, but all caught something of the young man's joy.

He said his name was Matthias, and since the time of his

visit to the child—some month and a few days earlier, he thought, though he didn't know exactly—he had told the story to many people who had scoffed at him and made fun of him. "I'm not a crazy man," he said defiantly. "I am not a drunkard. I saw the things I saw and in my heart I know they're true."

He told them where to find the inn. "But," he added, "the baby will surely no longer be there in the manger. By this time the census crowds have thinned, and some innkeeper or some kind person must have given them a place to live."

Melchior offered Matthias a reward for his information, but this the young shepherd refused. "I've had my reward," he said softly. Sunset was coming on, and he said he had to return to the fields. "One of us comes to the inn every day," he told them. "We speak of what we have seen. Today it was my turn. Thank you for believing me." He said farewell to them—even to Krampus, who stared at him as though the shepherd were some strange being that he did not quite recognize—and then the young man took up his shepherd's hook and walked away toward the hills.

The three kings were on fire to go, even before the star showed in the sky. Agios and Krampus barely had time for a hurried meal before they pushed on. A half-hour after sunset, the star glowed again, brighter than ever, though somehow it had changed.

It no longer looked like a star, Agios thought. It was almost like a human form, standing, impossibly, in the heavens. That might have been only illusion, though, for its radiance was such that he could glance at it only indirectly. It seemed lower, and, no question about it, the star *moved*. It went before them in the sky, floating as it seemed, leading them onward, always within sight above the roofs of the little town.

Not long after dark they arrived at the wall around Bethlehem. The Roman guards grumbled at them for arriving so late, but accepted a small bribe and grudgingly allowed them to pass through the gate. The guards took no notice of the star at all—perhaps, thought Agios, it was meant to be seen only by people looking for it.

They found themselves in a maze of narrow streets with modest buildings of stone or stone-and-plaster. The houses presented mostly sand-colored fronts broken only by a single doorway.

Agios supposed they would stop to ask directions.

He was wrong. Somehow they never lost sight of the star.

At last they came to an open market square with a trickling fountain at its center. Agios recognized on one side two Roman temples. Caspar saw him staring at them and explained, "One's dedicated to Jove, the chief Roman god. The other is a pantheon, a temple for worshipping all the others." Dim lights shone through the colonnades of both, eternal lamps kept at the altars by the priests and priestesses.

In the light of the star the temple lamps faded to gloom.

Shops lined two other sides of the square, and an inn took up the remaining side, opposite the Roman temples. The star beamed down from directly above the inn.

The sprawling building stood revealed in the radiance. Everything else lay in the shadows and the reflected glow. As they approached, with a suddenness that Agios could not at first comprehend, the star went out.

One moment its light poured down; the next it had vanished, with no sound, with no whisper of a breeze. Overhead the other stars shone in a clear sky. *The* star, though, for the first time in nearly a year, according to Melchior, had disappeared. He could hear no night sounds, no animals murmuring as they settled to sleep, no twitter of bats or swallows, no human footfall or voice.

"What does this mean?" Agios asked, and even in his own ears his voice seemed unusually loud.

Melchior said, "It means the star's task is finished," he said. "Look there."

Someone stood in the arched doorway of the inn yard. It was difficult to see in the sudden darkness, and Agios, remembering Matthias's story of the angels, felt his heart speed up.

However, the figure lifted a lamp, and it was only a man, somewhere between thirty and forty, with gray just beginning to streak his hair and his beard. He stepped toward the approaching strangers and waited. When they came near, he said, "I have been expecting you."

"Expecting us?" Melchior asked, sounding puzzled. "How could that be?"

"A messenger said you would come," the man said, using the same word, *malakh*, that the shepherd had.

Agios whispered to Melchior, "*Angelos*. The messenger he speaks of is an angel."

"Is—is the child—?" Melchior's voice choked in his throat.

The man smiled. "Come with me and see. My name is Joseph."

Chapter 8

They were not rich folk. The room they had been given was small and cramped, barely large enough for husband, wife, and child. The three scholar-kings crowded it, and Agios stood outside the doorway. Though he knew seeing the infant king would remind him of Philos—and though he dreaded it—he found himself drawn to the light that spilled from the small room. He had to restrain Krampus, who would have followed the scholars in. The misshapen man drew as close to the door as he could—and suddenly fell to his knees, staring.

Agios watched in puzzlement, feeling strangely disturbed. He got only occasional glimpses of the mother and her child, because the three men kept bending to gaze at them, blocking Agios's line of sight. To him the baby looked exactly like a baby, healthy enough, not much more than a month old, swaddled in plain linen and cradled asleep in his mother's arms. The small head was crowned with curly brown hair, the cheeks were pink, the features delicate.

Agios saw only a baby, not a king. And yes, he thought of Philos as he had been on the day of his birth, cradled in Weala's arms as she crooned to him. Agios's throat tightened.

Krampus rocked from side to side and made an inarticulate sound, a sound of yearning and of awe. Agios softly called him, but Melchior glanced back with a smile—and with tears shining on his face—and shook his head gently. Agios let Krampus stay where he knelt.

He stood near the doorway with his back to the room and listened as Caspar and Balthasar haltingly complimented the child, begged that their unworthy gifts be accepted by the parents, and knelt to honor the baby.

The child's mother spoke to them with great gentleness in her voice. They might have been her children, too—she had that air of motherhood about her, the kind of loving concern that Agios remembered seeing so often in Weala's eyes. In plain and homely language, Joseph thanked them for their kind words.

Then Melchior offered his praise and his adoration. When he rose to his feet, the kings presented their gifts, one after the other, and the mother wept and thanked them humbly.

Joseph had said her name was Mary, and the infant's name was Yeshua—Jesus, in the common tongue. Caspar and Balthasar murmured together of ancient prophecies. Agios caught the word "Immanuel," an old Hebrew word meaning "God is with us."

Melchior asked the couple if he and his friends might hear the account of the child's birth. Joseph said, "You tell them, Mary." In a soft and rather shy voice, she told a strange story—a story of being visited by, yes, an angel, who had told her she would give birth to a son, whom she must name Jesus. She was a virgin then, she told them, though betrothed to Joseph. The angel had said that the son she was to bear would be the son of God Himself.

Joseph took up the story: He, too, had been visited by the angel, who told him the truth of Mary's pregnancy, not a disgrace but an honor to her. He did not break their engagement, but married her, knowing she carried a child like no other in the world.

"I'm a carpenter in Nazareth," he finished. "But I'm of the house of David, and when we were ordered to register for the census, we had to come here to Bethlehem, the home of my ancestors. It was a difficult journey. Mary's time was close, and once here we could find nowhere to stay—the town was so crowded. No one had room."

Mary said, "Until the keeper of this inn, out of kindness and pity, said we might stay in the stable. It was a roof over our heads, and it was warm."

Joseph resumed: "And so our child was born in the manger of this inn. We saw signs and wonders at the time of his birth, and we know the story the angel told us is true."

They would have talked on, far into the night, but Melchior rose and urged his friends out. "They need their rest. Time enough tomorrow," he said. As he left, he turned back and said to Joseph, who stood in the doorway, "We have been commanded by King Herod to let him know of the child. The king himself!"

Joseph smiled. "We are going to Jerusalem in two days. The time has come for Mary's purification and for the child to be presented in the Temple there. If King Herod wishes, he can see Jesus then."

Melchior bowed and said, "We would consider it an honor to make the journey with you."

Joseph thanked him and then looked past Melchior and said, "Do you wish to see the baby?"

Krampus rose, turned, and shambled over to crouch behind Agios. He put his hand to his face and shook his head, weeping. Standing in the darkness, Agios felt his face grow hot. "He thinks he's too ugly," he explained. "He thinks he might frighten the child." He turned away quickly.

The kings were able to rent two rooms in the inn, one for the three of them and one for Agios and Krampus.

"Krampus won't sleep in a room," Agios said.

Krampus murmured, "Manger." He pointed in the direction of the stables. "I sleep there?"

Caspar said, "He heard the story. Now he wants to sleep where the baby was born. I think he feels close to the child."

Agios smiled. "A manger is something too small for you, Krampus. But we'll find you a bed of straw in the barn if you want." To Melchior, Agios said, "He's like a child himself."

"And he has the faith of a child," Melchior said softly. "I saw him kneeling. Of all the presents we came to offer, I think maybe Krampus offered the best."

"He gave nothing," Agios said.

"He gave his belief," Melchior corrected. "Let Krampus

go rest. You stay with us for a while, please. I'm sure we want to discuss what we have seen and heard. Sometimes when Caspar and Balthasar are enthusiastic, I can't understand one word out of five."

And so Agios found himself on a bench in their room—again a small room, hardly fit for men of their stature. The others were excited and talked far into the night, so rapidly that they were often hard to follow, and they spoke of ancient writings and signs and omens that Agios could not begin to understand. He did his best, though, and they shared enough knowledge for them, at least, to make sense of it all.

When the three kings had talked themselves out, they fell asleep from sheer exhaustion. Agios went into the room next to Melchior's and was the last to doze, and for some little time he lay on his back, listening to the steady breathing—and the snores—of the others, coming clearly through the wall. He smiled to himself in the dark. He had learned one thing, at least: even kings were men like other men. Balthasar's snoring was as loud as a lion's warning rumble.

Then it seemed to Agios that he had hardly closed his

eyes when he heard Melchior's urgent voice in the darkness: "Brothers!"

At the same instant Caspar began in his own language, "I dreamed—"

And in his, Balthasar gasped, "I've had a vision—"

Agios rose and went to the scholars' room, where they had lit a lamp. A moment later a troubled Joseph came, too, and asked to speak with them. Agios stood in a dark corner, the half-open door accidentally shielding him from Joseph's line of sight, and translated as best he could, though Joseph and the others had a hard time keeping patience, each wanting to tell the story first.

At last it began to sort itself out as Agios worked hard to keep up. All four men had dreamed the same thing, at the same instant: Melchior said, "I saw before me an angel, as Agios spoke of when he told us the shepherd's story—"

Balthasar broke in, overwhelmed with excitement: "I could have reached out and touched him! He shone, as the shepherd said, and he warned me—"

And Caspar: "He said we can't trust Herod. We have to make sure he doesn't hear about Jesus."

Joseph added in a grief-stricken tone, "Herod will kill

children to find our son! There is no safety in Bethlehem for us, or anywhere in Palestine."

In the sudden silence that followed, as Joseph and the three wise men stared at each other, Agios murmured softly, "I had no dream." He tried to say it as a simple matter of fact, but his voice trembled. The truth was that he felt left out, deprived. If he could only see an angel, maybe he could find belief, comfort, whatever had left him when Philos died. The thing that soothed Melchior's spirits and gave him a calm and peaceful serenity.

Melchior said finally but warmly, "Agios, my friend, I ask you to leave us."

"To leave you?" Now Agios felt as if he were being turned away from—from something wonderful. "Have I offended you, sir?"

With a smile, Melchior patted his shoulder. "Not at all. And it isn't that I don't trust you, Agios, for I look on you as I would a brother. I feel in my heart that with Joseph's help the three of us must make a difficult decision now. I promise we won't leave you out, but those of us who had the same dream must take the burden on our own shoulders. We'll make ourselves be calm as we discuss it and we'll understand each other well enough."

Agios went back to his room and dressed and then stepped out into the inn yard. The night was beginning to wane. Soon dawn would come in like a slow tide, paling the stars. Standing in the open yard, looking straight up beyond the dark fronds of the date palms, Agios saw only ordinary stars there, and a pale sliver of waning moon. Only fading, distant, indifferent stars—not *the* star.

"Why did the dream not visit me?" he asked the darkness, startled by the sorrow he heard in his own voice.

He sat on a bench and slumped against the wall of the inn, cool in the earliest morning hours. *When my agreement with Caspar ends, I will go back into the mountains*, he promised himself. *I will build a hut, nothing like my old one, but a different one where I won't look up and expect to see my wife and child . . . and I'll live there alone by trapping and hunting, live there far from people, alone, alone.*

Alone. Agios thirsted for solitude.

No. He couldn't have that. There was Krampus. Maybe he could find some place where the big man could stay without becoming an object of torture and scorn. Or Krampus could come with him—he was loyal, and he seldom spoke. Being with Krampus was almost like being alone, Agios thought.

He had known traders and kings, beggars and scholars, a tortured and twisted slave whose mind had been cracked by ill-treatment, and a shepherd boy who all seemed to have been given a great gift . . . and now a carpenter and his infant son. A carpenter who believed his child was actually the son of God.

All babies are children of God.

The thought had come into Agios's head from nowhere. In an anguished voice, he asked aloud, "Then why did Philos have to die so young? Why did God not take care of him for me?"

No answer came from the empty sky.

Then Agios heard the murmur of voices and stood up. Melchior, Caspar, Balthasar, and Joseph came out into the courtyard, mere silhouettes in the darkness. In the dim predawn light of the sky, Melchior beckoned to Agios as they walked to a far corner, where no one was likely to overhear them. "This is important," he said to Agios in a voice little louder than a whisper. "You must find the true words in the kind of Aramaic that Joseph speaks. There can be no mistake."

Agios nodded. "I understand."

Melchior was the spokesman. Through Agios's halting

translation, he told Joseph, "We have all had the same kind of vision. It had to be a sign. As you saw your angel, we saw ours, and his warning is plain. Your dream makes it certain: Herod intends evil for the child. You must keep him safe."

"How?" Joseph asked.

Melchior paused and then asked, "Are you determined to take the boy to Jerusalem?"

Sounding troubled, Joseph replied, "We must. Our religion tells us that it's the will of God. Yes, we must go to the Temple for Mary's purification and to present Jesus to God."

"If you must go, you must. However, travel secretly," Melchior said. "Tell no one of the . . . special circumstances of the boy's birth. Perform your rituals in the Temple as quickly and quietly as you can. Afterward, don't linger in the town, not even for a single night. You have to leave Jerusalem. Leave Judea."

"Where shall we go?" Joseph asked.

Melchior turned to Balthasar, who spoke, again through Agios's translation: "Take the child to Egypt. I know people there who will give your family shelter and protection. We will give you money for the trip. We will send messages to families we know who will take you in along the way and let you rest. I'll tell you how to find the first house, and the couple there will send you to the next along the way. In Egypt you can find work and begin to raise the boy."

Then Melchior again: "I have the feeling you and your family must stay hidden away for a long time—for a year or maybe even longer. You will know when it's time to return to your home, to Nazareth."

Joseph asked, "You are certain this is the only way?"

Melchior replied, "It seems best to us. We will help all that we can. The three of us plan to leave this morning and not return to Jerusalem at all, nor tell Herod of what we have learned and seen. His heart is dark, and we must keep Jesus safe from him."

Joseph's voice held worry: "The road to Egypt is a long journey, and it is a strange land. We will surely need more help."

"You *will* have help," Melchior said. "As I said, I'll send messages. You'll find friends along the way. They will be watching for you."

"I thank you," Joseph said.

"Go in to Mary. Prepare her for what must happen," Melchior said.

Joseph, still seeming uneasy, nodded and turned away.

When he had gone, Caspar took him aside and said quietly, "Agios, I have a task for you as well."

No, Agios thought.

He said nothing but waited.

Caspar said, "Agios, you must keep the child safe, above all else. I charge you to go with Mary, Joseph, and Jesus out of Judea and into Egypt. Take care that they do not know you are watching over them—that will be safer for them. I will give you money. Arm yourself so you and Krampus can protect them. Krampus may want to go near the child, but don't let him do that. His awe is too obvious, and his size might attract notice from people who would harm the child. You understand? Stay reasonably near Mary and Joseph, but don't seem to be a friend of theirs   don't even speak to them, but watch over them. Their safety depends on their being just a small family on a journey, and if word got out that they went with a guard, they would draw attention and be in great danger. Take care and guard them, but from some distance away until they have settled in Egypt."

The boy reminds me of my lost son. To see him, day after day, but not to approach him—Agios tried to keep the sorrow out of his voice when he asked, "Then what?"

"Then they will be safe and you will be free. You will be well compensated."

With a stirring of pride, Agios said, "I demand no money to help you, Caspar. You know that."

"It's a reward. Not a salary, nor yet a bribe," Caspar said. He looked keenly at Agios—the dawn was fast coming, and they could see each other's faces. Suddenly, he gripped Agios by both shoulders. "I owe you an apology, my friend. For how I threatened you that first day we met. For the fact that I allowed my men to take the frankincense from your cloak. Like Krampus, my excitement at the coming birth of the king made me heedless. Forgive me."

Agios shook his head. "You don't need my forgiveness. I would have done the same thing had I been in your position."

"No, you wouldn't." Caspar shook his head.

It was hard for Agios to remember those days full of longing, pain, and wine that didn't drown any of it. Gruffly, he said, "If you must hear it, I forgive you, then." He dropped his gaze. "If I failed you, forgive me, too. I am not the same man I was then."

Caspar inclined his head, a bow of sorts. "Neither am I. And you have not failed me, my friend."

Agios found no reply to that.

"I know what I am asking you," Caspar continued, meeting Agios's eyes again. "I know this is a mission like none you have ever had before. You are a troubled man, Agios. The best remedy for a restless spirit is having much to do. And keeping the child safe is the most important task you may ever perform."

Agios winced. He had already failed the most important task he had ever been given.

I buried my own son. How can I keep another man's son safe?

"Sometimes," Caspar nearly whispered, "peace comes with forgiveness. And sometimes forgiveness must be earned—not from other men, but from our own hearts and spirits. I don't know what sins you have on your conscience, Agios, or what despair burns within you. Do this task, though, and in it atone for whatever you think you have done. See if that will bring you peace at last."

"Very well," Agios said, his voice nearly as low and heavy as Krampus's.

"I trust you," Caspar said.

Agios hoped he deserved that trust.

Chapter 9

The fairly short trip north to Jerusalem had to be slow-paced, for Mary and the child could stand just so much of the broiling-hot, winding road. Agios and Krampus—who had disguised his misshapen form and face beneath a turban and long robes—always walked many dozens of steps ahead of them or behind them, keeping them just within earshot if they should cry out and always within sight, but never speaking to them or seeming to take notice of them.

Joseph would never have noticed them anyway, for he was too worried about his wife and child. Mary rode on a donkey, a placid gray animal that plodded on patiently for hours on end without resistance or complaint. Agios sensed that the young mother tried not to ask for pauses, but now and then she had to rest in the shade, drink some water, and nurse the child.

Krampus and Agios always loitered some distance away and Agios spoke offhandedly to other travelers at such times: How had the weather been in the north? Was Greek wine selling well in Jerusalem? What about wool?

Casual talk, roadside gossip, often led from one thing to another, from inconsequential things to information Agios really wanted. One man who had been hurrying south but who had stopped to rest spoke in low, anxious tones of King Herod, whose soldiers were asking everywhere about boys born within the past year.

"It's not a normal thing for a king to do," the man said, shaking his head. "Everyone's wondering what it means, and everyone's alarmed—especially the parents of those boys. Bad enough that the Romans forced everyone to travel to the towns of their ancestors for their census, but now the king of the Jews demands this foolishness."

He broke off and darted an apprehensive and guilty look at Agios. Such words could be very dangerous, even deadly.

"It's nothing to me. I'm not of this country," Agios assured him with a shrug. "Just passing through. My friend and I usually work as guards and guides for caravans."

They camped twice on the way, and camped early, for Mary and Joseph and the child needed the rest. In the long evenings Agios talked with Krampus—or instructed him in speech. Krampus was beginning to talk a little more, and he surprised Agios now and then—he comprehended more than he seemed to. Still he would not mention his family or his home.

On the first night of their camping, Agios asked Krampus to take the first watch and waken him when he wanted to sleep himself. That didn't happen, and Agios woke almost at sunrise to find Krampus still alert. "You let me sleep too long," he said.

Krampus smiled. "I watch. You sleep. You . . . need sleep more."

He is trying to give me a gift, Agios thought. He thanked the big man, but the next night he took the first watch. He woke Krampus at midnight.

They reached Jerusalem the next day, in the middle forenoon. As always, hopeful merchants had set up the usual maze of booths outside the gates and had even spilled some way inside the city. They shouted boasts about their goods, they implored passers-by to pause and look, and they offered everything from food—dried fish and fresh lamb, vegetables and fruits, wine and honey, goat's milk, cow's milk, butter and cheese, grapes, a dizzying assortment in fact—to clothing, shoes, weapons, medicines, magic potions, and more besides.

The noisy, jostling crowd was lucky for them, Agios thought. With all the commotion, the two quiet travelers Joseph and Mary would attract less attention. He and Krampus were some distance ahead of the family and reached the gates first.

The bored Roman guards were letting merchants and shoppers and idlers go in and out freely and didn't do more than glance at Agios and Krampus, but a gray-robed man standing near them, a man with the smugly official look of a king's servant, stopped a couple who were coming in. The woman carried a child, not even an infant but a toddler maybe two years old.

"Boy or girl?" the man asked.

The woman stared at him as if thinking only an idiot would ask that with the child in plain sight. "A girl. Her name is Rachel."

The official said in a fussy voice, "Show me she's a girl."

The couple looked at each other, but they seemed too timid to protest. The woman said, "She's just over two years old," and started to undress the child.

Before she had finished, the man waved them on. "That's enough, you can go. You could have told me sooner how old she was and that she's a girl."

The couple apologized—*Civilization*, Agios thought with contempt for the officious man with his insulting questions and his conviction that everyone but him was in the wrong—and the mother adjusted her daughter's clothes as they moved along. He muttered to Krampus, "Go and wait for me at the mouth of that alley. Stand quietly, as though waiting for someone, and speak to no one. No matter what you see or hear, wait for me to come to you."

Krampus shambled along, his robes hiding his ungainly form. He reached the alley and stood in the shade, arms folded, head down, as though patiently awaiting some friend or trader.

By that time Joseph and Mary had almost arrived at the gate, just behind Agios. Agios turned and cried out, "My old friend!" He lurched over to the official, speaking loudly like a lunatic or drunken man and embracing the gray-robed man in a bear hug, forcibly turning him so his back was to the gate. "I haven't seen you in years! You look just exactly the same as you used to. Phidias, how are you?"

The startled official struggled in Agios's strong grip. "Let go of me! I'm not—"

Agios spun him around in a quarter-turn as Joseph and Mary walked past just steps away. "Let me look at you!" Agios laughed, lifting the furious official momentarily off his feet, an outraged squirming fellow with all his attention on this bear of a bearded barbarian.

Agios set him down and pretended to brush dust from the shoulders of his robe. "You don't even recognize me, do you? No wonder! I was so thin in those days. And just look at how stout I am, and look at my beard! I didn't have this when we sat together on the seat of a Roman galley, did I? But tell me about yourself. You're so well-dressed, Phidias! You must've done well in the world, my old friend! How did you get your freedom?"

The man's face was scarlet. "I've never been a galley slave!"

"No shame in having once pulled an oar, Phidias!" Agios bellowed, laughing and thumping him on the shoulder so hard he made the official stagger. "Once you earn your freedom, you're equal to any Roman citizen! By Jove, Phidias,

I can see you've done well! A rich man, I'll wager. My old friend! Say, buy a drink for an old shipmate, will you?"

The two Roman guards were laughing. They sauntered over and one said, "Be off with you, fellow. You've made a mistake. This is a man from Herod's court, not a former slave."

Agios blinked as though trying to work that out. He saw that Mary, Joseph, and Jesus were now safely past and in the street, turning to the right and vanishing among the crowds. "Not Phidias Simonides? You look so much like him—no, I suppose he'd be much older than you are, not as good-looking. What a fool I've been! A thousand pardons, noble sir. Forgive a poor man's honest mistake. I meant no disrespect." He bowed low and stumbled off, the guards' laughter and the official's muttered curses following him.

As soon as he was out of sight of the gate, Agios picked up his pace, threaded his way through the crowds, and beckoned to Krampus. "You did well to keep your place, friend," he told the big man. "Come on." The two hurried through the crowds and came within sight of the small family Agios had sworn to protect. He trailed in their wake as they walked uphill to the Temple quarter of the city, where the enormous Second Temple dominated everything.

Agios saw Joseph and Mary approach its looming walls and speak to a man dressed in dark robes—a priest, he supposed. After a brief murmured conversation, he conducted them and the child up a broad sweep of steps on which hundreds of people milled, and then priest, husband, wife, and child vanished from Agios's sight as they went through a double gate.

Agios looked up—and up again, to the gilded roof far overhead.

"What?" Krampus asked him.

"This is the temple of their God," Agios explained. "Up there, somewhere, there's a special room, the Holy of Holies they call it. That's what I've heard from Jews I met in the caravans, anyway. It's so hallowed by their God that only priests can enter. They tell me that once it held a sacred relic."

"What is relic?" Krampus asked, his tongue stumbling over the unfamiliar word.

"I don't know. Anyway, the Jews say the first Temple that stood here was built by a king of old, a wise man like our three kings, a man named Solomon. The Babylonians, they say, sacked that temple and took away the treasures. This temple was built by Herod's father. Now the Holy of Holies has no treasure to protect."

Krampus grunted. "Holds memory," he said.

Agios stared hard at the misshapen man. Sometimes his simplemindedness had almost the sound of wisdom.

They waited. Agios didn't understand the rituals that the family would undertake, except that Jesus, as first-born son, was to be consecrated to the Lord. So Agios and Krampus kept their peace and shifted their position often, not wanting to attract any guard's attention.

Agios didn't speak to anyone, and if anyone spoke to him, he returned only a polite greeting and a nod. Agios was a nonbeliever, and he didn't know how strict the rules might be for a non-Jew. Maybe they would object to his being so close to the Temple. As for Krampus, he seemed to be invisible to the passers-by—that, or some indefinable threat about his gigantic stature and his muffled form made them keep their distance.

A man in a crowd who does not talk overhears many things. Agios listened to fearful low conversations about Herod and his census of childbirths—what could it mean? Were the Romans behind it? More trouble for the city? No one knew for sure.

Together with Krampus, Agios moved from place to place, gazing around while keeping one eye on the Temple steps. From here he could see much of the city of Jerusalem, its newest buildings toward the north. Looking east he saw hills—though he overheard a man, showing the place to visitors from out of town, call them mountains. One he heard called the Mount of Olives, a roundish mound planted thick with the fanlike shapes of olive trees. Its height made it little more than a knoll to Agios, nothing to the towering rugged mountains where he had been born and raised.

They waited until the hour before sunset, with Agios starting to worry that something had gone wrong. Then with great relief he recognized Joseph, and then beside him Mary, carrying her child. They were coming slowly down the wide steps, an old man at Joseph's elbow, taking only one slow step down at a time. Agios saw that he trembled as he walked—but then he realized that the old man was also weeping, blinded with tears.

Agios did not so much as look twice at Joseph and Mary, but he fell in not far behind them. The old man—Agios heard Joseph call him "Simeon"—was saying, "Now the Lord may let me go in peace. He promised me that I would not die until I had seen and held in my arms this child, who will bring salvation to Israel and to the Gentile world

145

alike." He murmured prayers of thanks and blessing and said his farewell as Joseph and Mary left the temple gates.

When Agios was certain that no one was paying the least attention—crowds still thronged the streets in the fading heat of the long day—he came up behind Joseph and said, "Don't look around, Joseph. I'm one of the friends Melchior promised would help you. Have you performed all of your rites?"

"Yes," Joseph said, not even twitching his head to look.

"Then leave the city now. Herod is searching for your child. There is a stable on the left a few yards past the Bethlehem Gate. I'll hurry ahead there, and when you come to it, ask and they will have animals ready for you. If you're asked about the child, tell them the baby is a newborn, just three days old. Say you're from some other town, not Bethlehem or Nazareth, and that the child wasn't born in Galilee."

Agios took Krampus's arm as they came to a side street and pulled him down it. They threaded their way to the gate and then out into the market plaza. Agios estimated that they had only minutes to make things ready. Agios paused to make hurried purchases at the booths—bread, dried fruit and meat, warm blankets, and other goods.

Then they reached the stable, where business was slow, and Agios called the owner aside and bargained.

Dipping into the purse of money that Melchior had given him, Agios bought two healthy-looking mules, one for Joseph to ride and one to bear supplies, as well as blankets and a packsaddle. He and Krampus loaded the pack mule with the food and other supplies. While Agios and Krampus had waited near the Temple, he had learned from people he asked casually that the best way to Egypt was the Sea Road, one of the Romans' splendidly engineered routes.

He wondered if the family would be safe going that way, or even after they arrived. Egypt, of course, was still part of the Roman Empire—along the shores of the Mediterranean there was no escaping Roman control—but it was at least far beyond the limits of Herod's power. Hoping that Herod did not wield enough influence to pursue them beyond the boundary of Judea, Agios pointed out Joseph and Mary to the stable owner as the couple came into view, still within the gates.

The fussy government official whom Agios had hailed as his old friend was no longer on duty, but another, older and fatter but otherwise almost interchangeable with him, stood in his place, shifting from foot to foot as if he had grown tired of this duty.

"Where is your home?" the man asked Joseph in an officious voice.

Joseph's reply was too soft for Agios to hear. He and Krampus sauntered toward the gate, just in case.

But scrutiny of those leaving the city was not as strong as it was for arrivals, and the official gestured for Joseph and Mary to go on. They made their way out of the gate, saw the stable, and made their way over to it. The owner, aware that Agios and Krampus loitered nearby, gave them the animals that Agios had purchased.

Mary looked frightened and held the child close to her heart.

Then the family moved on, out to the southbound road, Joseph riding the saddled mule and leading the second one, loaded with enough provisions to see them well away from the city.

Mary's sturdy donkey set the steady pace southward. They continued that first night until even Joseph looked ready to drop from exhaustion, and then they found refuge with shepherds who had camped on a hillside nearby. Agios and Krampus passed the shepherd camp and stopped for the night beneath a cluster of date palms not far off the road.

They rested a few hours, then Krampus nudged Agios awake and muttered, "They leave." Joseph and Mary had risen before the sun and continued to make their way southward. The sun rose and shone hotter and hotter until again they were forced to pause and snatch a few hours of rest.

Their route eventually led them toward Gaza, where they would find the Sea Road that would lead them down and into Egypt. Ahead lay the long stretch of Sinai, the southwestward-curving eastern shore of the Mediterranean. The weather grew so dangerously hot that by the middle of each morning they always rested in shade, emerging only when evening brought cooling breezes. Agios and Krampus took care to keep them within sight—but to remain inconspicuous themselves.

They traveled faster in the early hours after sunset, stopping when full darkness fell, when they camped or stayed with hospitable, humble folks—Melchior's network of helping families, Agios supposed. They resumed the journey in the hours just before dawn until the sun climbed high enough to become an agony.

Agios thought they were almost away from Judea and from Herod's grasp, until one evening as he saddled his own mule, two men came riding horses into the village where they had passed the night. It was the hour of the evening meal, and few people were out—but even they retreated indoors at the sight of the two armed men.

Joseph and Mary had already started on their way, but the two riders had their eyes on the couple. They paused near Agios, and one of them spoke to him in Latin, the language of the Romans: "Is that a Jewish child?" He pointed at the couple ahead, Joseph riding slowly to keep pace with the little donkey, far too slowly for two soldiers on horseback to worry about whether they might get away.

Agios, ready to mount his own mule, acted stupid: "What child?"

The guard pointed. "That couple has a child! Male, is it?"

"Oh, them," Agios said. "A girl child. They're Egyptian, those two. Nice young couple. They had to make a pilgrimage; one of their relatives died near here and they—"

Herod's soldier insisted: "We don't need the whole story. Might the child be a boy? We have orders to return all Jewish male babies to Jerusalem."

Agios still tried to delay them, standing and holding on

to the reins of the soldier's horse. "It's a girl," he insisted. "I don't speak Egyptian, but I know a girl when I see one."

"Drop the reins!" the commander snapped.

Agios pretended not to understand. "The inn a mile ahead has good red wine, gentlemen, if you're thirsty——"

The older man leaped from his saddle, drew his gladius, the short Roman sword, and tried to shove Agios aside.

Agios seized his arm, grappled with him the way he had once grappled with a dying bear, and with the same desperation. The man seemed surprised by his iron grip—Agios looked older than he was, and no one could guess that a heavy man like him had so much speed in him, so much muscle and so much determination.

"Let go!" the angry soldier spat. "I'll have your head! Absalom, help me deal with this fool!" He tried to bring his sword up, but Agios kept him in too tight a grip, and he had no room, no chance to stab.

The second, younger soldier dismounted and strode forward, drawing his own sword, and danced as Agios spun the other man. The younger soldier's face showed his confusion and distress.

His commander shouted, "Kill him!" as he twisted savagely in Agios's grip. Agios put a foot against the man's left heel, pivoted, and swung, and the younger man's sword chopped into the back of his senior's neck with a sickening sound.

The body went limp, the spine severed, and the man, his eyes wide in anger and shock, did not even cry out. Something invisible left his body, and suddenly Agios held dead weight.

Agios feinted, avoiding another sword blow, and then thrust the body forward, using him as a shield. The second man panicked at the sight of the dead soldier, tried to push the bleeding body away from him, forgetting about the sword in his hand.

And then Krampus stepped from the shadows and seized the man's sword arm, immobilizing him. Agios landed a solid blow in his face, one that cut his forehead and sent him stumbling backward. He tried to rise—

But Krampus hauled him up instead, grasping the straps of his breastplate, and he lifted him as easily as Mary would have picked up her child. The frightened young soldier squeaked, his heels dangling.

Agios said in a language the man could understand, "You've killed your captain. For that they'll cut your guts out! These people and their baby are nothing to you. And look—no villager has come to help you. They don't like you here, you know? I'm taking your weapon—do you understand me? Ships pass this way all the time. If I were you, I'd board one of them heading to Greece or to Rome. Better that than to face the anger of your king Herod! Krampus, put this man down."

Krampus did, and the soldier looked up into the big man's twisted face, the mouth agape, eyes glaring. The soldier screamed.

"Shush," Agios said. "When you wake up, think over what I told you."

He struck one more sudden blow, one that sent the second man into a sleep from which he'd wake with an aching head—and maybe a wiser one. Mary and Joseph were already out of sight. Agios collected both swords, tied them into place on his mule's burden, and mounted one of the soldiers' two horses.

With Krampus leading the other horse and the mule, they hurried after the family they were guarding, but when they came within sight of the sea they stopped. Agios dismounted and slapped both horses on the haunches to send them running, and then waded into knee-deep water and threw both swords spinning as far as he could. They splashed into the Mediterranean and sank.

He had blood on his hands, broken skin on his knuckles. The salt water burned as it washed the traces away. Agios wondered what Caspar might think of this. He had killed one of Herod's men—or at the very least had been present at his death, which would amount to the same thing if he were caught.

He was committed now. He could not go back, not through Judea. Nor could Krampus, who would, in Roman eyes and those of the king of Judea, share his guilt.

They hurried on their way and soon came within sight of a distant Joseph and Mary. When they reached the frontier, they saw none of Herod's men. Only Romans guarded the way. If they'd had any orders from the Jewish king Herod, they didn't seem to think they were serious enough to worry about. They waved the travelers through.

One moment they were on the fringe of Herod's realm, the next they had stepped beyond his reach. Agios gave a sigh of relief.

It was still a long way to Egypt, but now, Agios thought,

they had at least a good chance of making it there safe and alive.

Neither Joseph nor Mary knew of the soldiers. *Let it be my burden*, Agios thought. *They have more than enough trouble of their own.*

He and Krampus drew ahead of the family. They entered the land of Egypt on a burning hot day that made the air shimmer so that the buildings and palm trees ahead seemed to writhe and dance. The people's language was strange, but Agios was able to understand and be understood. Balthasar had said that Joseph and Mary were to find a man in Alexandria, the port city founded by and named for Alexander the Great. He would have received letters and money by now, and he would be able to help them.

When Joseph and Mary crossed a wide river, they did not seem to notice Krampus and Agios watching on the far shore. But the two men didn't stop following the couple and their baby until they had found the man Balthasar had told them of. From there the little family traveled south to Memphis, a city filled with great temples and brightly painted tombs dating back into the earliest memories of mankind. Though Agios couldn't take full credit for their escape, he took some solace in knowing that Jesus would have a chance to grow into a boy and then a man.

Caspar had hinted that in helping the family Agios would find solace.

He felt none of it. True, he had seen the infant Jesus to a place of safety, but he felt no relief in the fact.

For what he had done for another child was more than he had done for his own son.

Chapter 10

With Mary and Joseph safely in Egypt, Agios found himself at a loose end. It was hard to believe the path his life had taken, and even more incredible to imagine going forward. He had no home, no wife, and no son. And any fledgling hope that had sparked in the light of the star they had followed for so many sleepless nights was already pale and fading.

However, he had Krampus.

The simple man wanted to stay close to Jesus, but Agios wouldn't hear of it. Instead, he found a place away from the city where they could settle for a time to get their feet beneath them while Agios decided where they would go from here. Whether he liked it or not, his days would be filled with the burden of Krampus. Their lives were bound together.

Some distance away from the broad river that Mary and Joseph had crossed lay a wide, shallow valley surrounded by sandstone cliffs. Here and there the rock had been worked, carved by ancient hands: bas-relief gods or kings gazed out toward the Nile. In other places, water trickling for eons had worn caves into the stone. A cluster of these gave home to lepers, outcasts who suffered from a terrible disease that ate through flesh like slow fire.

Hermits occupied other caves, men who contemplated the stars or the gods and who seized time alone to do their thinking. A half-day's walk south from the city of Memphis, near a village of boatmen and farmers, Agios had found one empty cave, not a very impressive one, that served as shelter for him and for Krampus. With money that Caspar had given them, Agios bought some goats. Krampus delighted in them. He learned the simple tasks of leading them out to pasture and later returning them to the cave, where Agios had built a pen for them.

The days blended into one another until a full year passed. Then one day in the village marketplace, Agios overheard an agitated man's voice: "It's true! It's terrible, but it's true. All of them! Scores, maybe hundreds!"

A woman asked, "Herod killed *children?*"

Agios shouldered through the crowd. A cluster, mostly women and a few men, stood around a man dressed in the clothing of Judea, his expression grim. "Yes!" the man, short and scrawny, said. "He was afraid of some prophecy—one of the children was to grow up and overthrow Herod or something. Herod sent his soldiers in and they hacked them to pieces, every single boy born in Bethlehem for two years past!"

Some of the women were sobbing. One of the Egyptian men said, "The Romans won't let him remain king. They can't. That's the act of a madman, a barbarian!"

Sick at heart, Agios turned away. *Scores, maybe hundreds.*

Every victim a child, a boy. Like Philos. Like Jesus.

Agios felt his heart grow stone-heavy. For many days he did not return to the village but stayed in the cave, staring out toward the Nile, though seeing nothing. His hands, as if working on their own, carved at a small piece of sandalwood. He hardly even glanced down. The knife shaved the wood tenderly, as though it were a living thing, as if the knife itself knew what must be taken, what had to remain.

The figure that his blade released from the bit of wood was not much bigger than his thumb, but it grew perfect: a tiny sleeping baby, curled up in a manger. A symbol. Perhaps it represented one of the children who had suffered and died, one of the victims of evil.

He will be King of Kings.

Agios closed his eyes, though his hands did not cease their work. If only it were possible for a king to offer mankind the way out of such cruelty, such wickedness. The three scholars had believed it would be so. They had faith.

No, Agios thought. *I can't share their confidence, their belief. I've seen too much of men and know too much of their twisted hearts. What can one small child offer against such hopelessness?*

Agios had no appetite and neglected to prepare meals, so each day Krampus cooked, after a clumsy fashion, and brought Agios scorched meats that he ignored. The big man tried to comfort him, even cutting the meat into bite-sized pieces. To placate him, Agios occasionally ate a mouthful or two.

At nights Agios lay sleepless, afraid to give in to the darkness of his dreams. Still, time began to wear away at his fears, as the Nile had carved itself a bed over unimaginable centuries. Gradually he began to recover, and he and Krampus resumed their quiet way of life.

One evening when Krampus returned with the goats, Agios gave him dinner. The big man ate gratefully. Afterward, as they had done over the past months, Agios encouraged Krampus to talk.

That evening Krampus surprised him. "You sad," he said. "Who you miss? Who die?"

"My wife. My son," Agios said quietly. Tears came to his eyes.

Krampus watched him and then said, "My father—I not know. Dead. My mother bake bread. To sell, to live. One day Romans come. They—" He broke off with a sob.

"You don't have to talk about it," Agios said.

Krampus wiped his tears with his big palm. "They— hold her down, tear off clothes. They—hurt her. And kill her. And take me from her. I would have—" he mimed stabbing. "They beat me. Every day. Then—" he imitated pulling an oar. "Chains. Slave. I want to die. Try to die. Then you come." His big hands fumbled in the air. "Don't know the words. You—me—we sorrow. But easier together."

He had never spoken so much all at one time. Agios repeated, "Easier together." Somehow it felt true.

And so as far as it could, Agios's grief slackened. A day even came when he renewed his trips to Memphis—half a day there, half a day back—and his trading. He heard nothing of Herod's being punished for his murder of the children. Perhaps the Romans did not care enough about these people on the fringes of their empire to concern themselves with such a small matter as the deaths of children.

One late afternoon as Agios was returning from Memphis and nearing their cave, he heard Krampus shouting from near the river. Agios ran there, and when he saw what was going on, fury rose within him.

Three laughing young boatmen ware dancing around Krampus, shouting at him, making fun of his ugliness. They held boat poles, ten feet long, and kept swinging them, sweeping Krampus's legs from under him, or running up and prodding him with them, wielding the poles like blunt spears. A shattered earthenware jug told Agios that Krampus had just come to the river for water. The boatmen must have pulled over for a meal or a rest—their reed boat had been moored to a palm tree on the bank.

Agios shouted, and they spun to face him. Krampus, bloody and scratched, scrambled away on all fours before rising to his feet. One of the three dodged toward him, raising his boat pole, and Krampus roared in anger.

"Leave him alone!" Agios bellowed. "He wasn't hurting you!"

"Look how ugly he is," another one of the three men jeered. "He's hurting our eyes!"

Snarling, Agios strode forward. The three turned on him, menacing him with their poles. "Back away, old man!" the one who seemed to be their leader warned.

When Agios didn't retreat, the three charged him. Agios ducked a blow—the boy swinging the pole gasped at his unexpected speed—then snatched up a fist-sized rock and sent it whistling into the second one's stomach, sending him flailing backward until he fell into the river.

He had dropped his pole, and Agios grabbed it. He parried a blow from the third, then cracked him over the head. Now only one boy stood, and he looked fearful and uncertain.

"Stop!" Krampus begged. "Not kill."

"They might have killed you!" Agios roared, his voice furious.

"Not evil for evil," Krampus said.

The three had retreated a few steps. Agios drew his bronze knife and strode to the tethered boat. With one swipe he cut the rope, then used the pole to send the craft into the river, where the current took it. "If you want it, go get it!" Agios said. "And never come here again."

The three boys cursed, but went splashing into the river, half-wading and half-swimming. Agios threw the pole after them. "Probably the boat belongs to their father," he growled. "They'll be in trouble if they don't—"

He broke off as he realized that Krampus had fallen to his knees, head bent, one fist against the rocky ground and the other hand clutched over his chest.

"Krampus!" Agios caught him about the shoulders and lowered him carefully to the sand. The muscles in Krampus's arms were hard as stones, his knuckles white in their iron grip. "Where are you injured?"

But Krampus couldn't respond. He gasped for breath. His eyes were wide and full of panic, his mouth open in a grimace of pain and fear. Frantic, Agios ran his fingertips over his friend's body, assessing the scratches and bruises that the boys from the boat had inflicted. The wounds were nothing that could cause such distress. The big man's lips were turning blue, and as Agios watched he squeezed his eyes shut. A single tear escaped and slid down his broad cheek.

Gripped by dread, Agios knelt beside Krampus. "Help my friend," he said—though the boatmen were gone, far out in the river, and no one else was around to hear. "Don't let my friend die."

I'm . . . praying, Agios thought. He had seen the three kings pray often, but it wasn't something he had ever done before, and he didn't know to which god he was muttering. "Hear me," he murmured. "If there is anything good and holy in the light that led us to the place where Jesus lay in his mother's arms, let it help us now."

Then he felt a hand cover his own. His eyes flew open to find Krampus staring at him. His hand trembled, but there was a small smile on his tear-stained face.

"What happened?" Agios croaked.

Krampus took Agios's hand and held it over his chest. His heart was pounding furiously. But even as he feared for his friend's life, Agios could feel the beats beginning to slow. He kept his hand over the place until the pace nearly matched his own and the color began to seep back into Krampus's pale cheeks.

"Has this happened before?" Agios asked.

Krampus nodded. "When . . . sometimes. When Romans beat me," he whispered.

"Are you better? Are you well?" But of course he wasn't well. Why hadn't Agios realized it before? Whatever had touched Krampus's body and face had clearly marked him inside, too. Who could know how Krampus suffered? How broken he really was?

"I'm sorry," Agios said, because there was nothing else to say.

"Better," Krampus grunted. Carefully, Krampus sat up and Agios helped him to his feet. Together they hobbled back to their cave, where Agios bandaged Krampus's cuts. There was nothing he could do for the wound in his heart.

So Agios and Krampus lived day to day, month to month, year to year, almost like a man and his over-large, ungainly son. From then on, though, when Agios made his trips into Memphis he cautioned Krampus to remain alone and quiet in the cave—and he made sure that the water urns were filled before he left.

On rare occasions, no more than once a year if that, messengers came and found Agios, bringing letters from Caspar or from Melchior, inscribed on tablets of wax in the Roman way. They wrote simply, for though Caspar had taught Agios the art of reading and writing, his grasp of educated language was weak. Melchior told him of how Balthasar fared. All three men held within them an eagerness to share word of the holy child born to become the King of Kings—but all agreed to hold back from telling the world of their secret, because, as Melchior wrote, "His time has not yet come, but I pray that I live to see it."

Then one day, a message arrived that turned their simple world upside down.

Herod is dead, Melchior had written. *I am sending word to Joseph that it is safe for him, Mary, and Jesus to return to their homeland now. My friend, will you accompany them home?*

It didn't even cross Agios's mind to say no.

They had little to pack. Agios had carved dozens of tiny figures over the years. They all fit in one large goatskin sack. When they went into the town to sell their herd, Agios carried the sack slung over his shoulder, and as they traveled, every time they saw a child, he left one of the little carvings for him or her to find. Krampus once tried to retrieve one of the carvings from a jeering ten-year-old, pointing and saying, "Bad boy!"

His voice scared the boy, who ran away. "What did he do?" Agios asked.

"Laugh at me," growled Krampus. For all his size and

fierce appearance, he really was like a child, with feelings that could easily be hurt.

With a sudden inspiration, Agios handed Krampus the little baby he had sculpted. "Here," he said. "This one is yours. You keep it forever."

Krampus stooped over and cradled the tiny figurine in his huge palm. "Oh," he said. "Oh." He looked up. Tears streamed down his cheeks. "Oh."

"I didn't mean to make you sad," Agios said gently.

"Him," Krampus said. "It is him. I see." He raised his cupped palm and held the little carving close to his heart. "He take Krampus home."

Agios shook his head. Krampus had ways of thinking that—well, that no one could really follow. At least, he couldn't.

They finished their business, Agios gave away all of his little toys, and they bought a camel. Instead of taking passage by boat—Agios worried about what Krampus would do if people made fun of him when they couldn't get away—they took the road that led north near the banks of the river.

In the marketplaces of Memphis Agios asked about news from Judea. What Melchior had written was true: Herod had died of an agonizing illness, people said, and because he had executed his oldest son before that, there was no clear successor to the throne. Instead, Herod's kingdom was split into three parts, each ruled by one of his surviving sons—Archelaus over Judea. The name meant nothing to Agios.

He and Krampus searched for Joseph and learned where he now lived. Agios did not approach him, but watched until he was sure, and then he told Krampus, "Melchior said in his message that they will leave soon. We'll go and make sure they are safe."

"We will see Jesus?" Krampus asked, his face shining.

"From a distance," Agios said.

Preparations for the move took some time. Joseph and Mary had celebrated Passover before all the purchases could be made. This time Joseph bought a horse for himself, a fine Arabian animal that seemed to have great stamina. Mary, it appeared, would ride the same placid donkey as before. They had kept the animal, and once before Agios had seen Mary walking beside it with Jesus, now four years old, mounted upon its back, clinging to its mane.

Agios had long since sold his mule, but he bought another, a strong animal though not as obedient as the first, as he and Krampus discovered the day after they set out. They had gone a distance of nearly twenty miles, all of it at a steady walk interrupted by a few periods of rest, when the mule decided that his workday was over. No amount of persuasion could change the animal's mind, so Agios and Krampus camped while Joseph and Mary went ahead.

However, Agios had begun to relax a little. He realized that Melchior must have again arranged for Joseph to find friends along the way—he and Krampus had seen the little family stop at a house, and Agios knew that others waited to help them with food and shelter, just as they had years ago. And of course Herod was dead now. They did not need to be as closely guarded as before.

The way back was a slow trip for Agios and Krampus— a full month from Alexandria up the Sea Road into Judea and then into Galilee. As before, Agios always rode a little ahead or a little behind Joseph and Mary, though with his mule's stubbornness sometimes interrupting the trip, sometimes he did not see them for a day at a time. Mary and the boy had to rest often, though, and Agios always had a good sense of whether the family was ahead or behind him, so he and Krampus matched their pace and they always saw the family again eventually, somewhere in the distance.

Once a week, beginning at sunset on Friday and until sunset on Saturday, the family had to pause. A Jewish merchant had explained the Sabbath to Agios already, back in Egypt. No devout Hebrew could work or travel on that day. If they were near a temple, the family went there. If no temple was available, they prayed where they were.

When at last they passed into Galilee, walking steadily north, Agios thought it a good country, a flat plain with mountains to the west and more distant ones off to the east. Broad fields of young rye and barley stood lush and green, and the olive groves were heavy with their ripening fruit. Years ago, when they had passed through similar countryside on their search for the King of Kings, Melchior had remarked to Agios and his friends, "This is a blessed land."

That was easy enough to believe when Agios saw the bounty of the fields and felt the friendliness of the people. Easy enough until he thought of the senseless murder of innocent children whose only offense was having been born in or near Bethlehem. A people who would consent to such insane laws made him doubt they were men at all.

And that led him to wonder: Melchior, Balthasar, and Caspar had assured him that this child was to be a King of

Kings, someone whose name would go forth through the whole world. But—a son of a carpenter?

Was the boy fated to become a warrior at the head of a conquering army? Was he to be a killer of men? How else could such a boy become a king?

Agios even began to doubt his memories. The star—did that really happen? The talk of angelic messengers—whom he'd never seen—could such visions only be dreams and delusions?

He did not speak of his misgivings, and Krampus seemed to have perfect faith. He often spent the evenings just staring in rapt devotion at the little carving Agios had given him. At such times his face was so peaceful, so joyful, that it was almost transfigured, almost handsome.

But Jesus, the boy Jesus—a King of Kings? Joseph and his people believed in only one God. Every other religion that Agios had learned about worshipped many gods, some of them fierce and dangerous to humans. What kind of god would this child follow? A god of war, of bloody battles?

Agios began to hope that the scholars from the east had been self-deceived, that it was all a mistake. Better for Jesus to live and die as a simple carpenter than as a king ordering the deaths of men, the enslavement of women and children. The more he pondered, the more the world darkened in his vision.

Nazareth turned out to be a white city perched on a hill, its stones shining in the morning sun. Compared to Alexandria and Memphis, it was small, but it obviously held a great place in Joseph's heart, and in Mary's.

They first stayed with a kinsman of Joseph's, while Joseph arranged to reopen his carpenter's shop. Joseph found a house, not large or ostentatious, but comfortable. They moved in and Agios told himself, *Now I can go. I've seen them to Egypt and back again. Whatever happens to the boy, whatever he becomes, is none of my concern. My promise to Melchior has been fulfilled.*

Yet somehow he stayed on. Krampus wanted to be near the family. Agios knew that if he insisted, Krampus would move on with him, but—*One place is as good as another*, he told himself. Agios bought a small flock of sheep, and he and Krampus became shepherds, living in a small hut a few miles from Nazareth, among gently rolling hills. Krampus became as good with the sheep as he had been with the goats in Egypt, and they resumed their quiet way of life, Agios and his adopted, ugly son, who inside was as gentle, and as simple, as a little child.

Chapter 11

Years passed and the world changed. Agios had reported the family's safe return to Nazareth in a
letter to Melchior. He had no response for a long time.
The Romans did not like unrest in Judea, and after two
years the emperor Augustus abruptly dismissed and exiled
Herod's son, decreeing that from then on Judea would
cease to be a kingdom, but would be combined with Syria
and Galilee into one Roman province.

That hardly mattered to the ordinary citizens, for life
went on as always. A full five years after the change of government, Agios at last received a message from Melchior

that saddened him: Caspar and Balthasar had both died, the former from a fever, the latter from a fall. "I am ill and may pass soon myself," Melchior said in the letter. "If I do, I will thank God that I was allowed our journey and our meeting the King of Kings. Farewell, Agios, and for the last time, perhaps, thank you." Agios wished that he had been able to say farewell to his old companions.

A score of years and more passed, while Agios and Krampus settled into a routine in their hut a few miles from Nazareth. The life of shepherds meant that they remained in the fields with the sheep during the dry months, lived in the hut during the rainy season—and each year, in the spring, found a shepherd boy to watch the flock while they undertook a journey that led through Nazareth, where they heard news of Jesus as he grew.

They heard of his being wise beyond his years, of his discoursing with learned teachers—rabbis, the Jews called such men—but they never once saw him. Still, on their annual trading journey they always passed through Nazareth, and almost every year they heard a little more.

For the rest of the time, Agios took care of their work and their meals, sometimes adding to their diet by going hunting in the hills around for small game, or fishing in the streams. On some days when he was in the forest or wading in a stream with a sharpened spear, watching for fish, he felt fleeting touches of peace.

Those were the times when he was alone, far away from petty kings or Roman laws, when he had no one to watch over or protect. He was free, in a way—though memories always came to keep him company, and then he would sigh and go back to the way of life he and Krampus had made for themselves. Routine could at least dull his aching need for solace.

Most of the time, though, he felt restless. He felt a constant urge to leave this place of shepherds and towns, to go back to the wild mountains, to spend his last years near the place where Philos had died—for he felt that time was passing and that, like all men, he was aging. Krampus certainly was. Though he was fifteen or more years younger than Agios, he had begun to walk with difficulty, leaning on a staff. Perhaps his insistence on sleeping in the open was causing it, or his weak heart, or perhaps it was merely the years passing.

Krampus was a man, and he would one day grow old and die. He occasionally had gasping fits like the one that happened in Egypt. After so many years, Agios knew that these episodes weren't painful so much as they were distressing—Krampus would sleep for hours afterward, his body weak with a weariness that clung to him for days. It frightened Agios, for he was also a man—he would pass, too. What would become of Krampus if Agios died first?

These thoughts invariably put Agios in mind of his son. At times he felt that Philos was near him, separated only by the thinnest of veils—but more often he was sure the boy was gone forever. He yearned to join his son in whatever waited beyond the grave, peace or oblivion.

To keep his mind and his hands occupied, Agios still carved and shaped things, but now, with wood and other materials more easily available, he had begun to make more intricate things: a Roman trireme with oars that moved all together; an Egyptian chariot drawn by a horse, the horse's hooves on small concealed wheels, and the chariot moving by means of a coiled brass spring that could be wound by turning the wheels backward; and intricate carvings of the animals he had seen in his travels: camels who lowered their necks as though drinking, alligators with snapping jaws like those he had seen in the Nile, bears, lions, even apes and monkeys.

These he stored until one of his annual visits to the surrounding villages, when he would distribute them to the children—or to the children traveling with their parents whom he passed on the road. Krampus would always mope when the shelves had been emptied, but soon Agios began to fill them again, and Krampus never lost the little carved baby that seemed to mean so much to him. When no other carvings remained in their hut, Krampus would sit in the sun and admire his own possession, looking at it as if it were wrought of gold, not of sandalwood, gazing at it as though every time he saw it anew. It comforted him when Agios gave away the other toys.

One spring, Agios had a large load to trade—not only dried and salted meat, but cheeses, many sheepskins, bags of wool, small leather bags of aromatic herbs for healing and cooking, and, of course, toys to place where children would find them. Their trading route usually took them in a lopsided circle from Nazareth to Jerusalem and back again. Agios liked to loop east before spending a few days in Jerusalem, where he would sell the bulk of his goods. Then he and Krampus would head home via a more direct route. There was little left for them to trade by the time they journeyed through Samaria, and though Agios didn't dislike the Samaritans the way the Jews did, he was content to travel through their country and back home quickly.

"Wear your loose robes and wrap your turban around your head," Agios reminded Krampus as they prepared. "Remember to be quiet, even if people yell at us. Their words can't hurt. Let me do all the talking."

Krampus nodded. "I know." Together he and Agios finished loading the camel, which was being unusually skittish. Agios, worried about Krampus and the journey ahead, perhaps did not pay as close attention to the animal as he should have.

They set off. It was a hot morning, and the camel, no longer young, took its time. By the end of the first day, the animal began to limp, favoring its right front leg. Agios paused to look at its foot but saw nothing wrong.

All the same, he decided to alter their route—to go directly to Jerusalem instead of meandering through the smaller hamlets along the way. Sychar in Samaria was only another half-day's journey, and Agios knew they could stop there if they needed to.

It proved to be a wise decision. By afternoon the beast was limping so badly they could no longer drag it along. Agios led the halting camel slowly and carefully to a shady spot, and there he stopped to look closely at the lame leg. Some insect had bitten it, he realized, on the inside of the right knee. A gall-sore as big as a fig had swollen, and pus seeped from it. "This has to be drained and bandaged," Agios told Krampus.

Camels have minds of their own, and this one was no exception. Krampus held the reins and kept the camel still as best he could. Agios carefully nicked the swelling with the tip of a sharp knife, making the camel surge and jerk, but the sore began to drain. When the discharge had turned bloody, showing that the bad humors had been purged from the swelling, Agios prepared a poultice of calendula leaves—some of the herbs he had intended to trade—and bound it to the animal's leg. The camel snorted and fidgeted, but seemed to be in less pain.

"Stay and mind him," Agios told Krampus. "I'll bring water."

They had used the well at Sychar often enough before. People called it Jacob's Well, after an ancient Jewish patri-arch who once had lived in the area. Agios untied a leather bucket and a long rope from the camel's pack.

The sun rode bright and white in a clear sky, not even a wisp of cloud offering protection from the unforgiving heat. Agios could feel sweat running down his neck and back, and he breathed shallowly as he climbed the hill to the place where the cistern offered relief. As he crested the short ridge, he saw no one else at the well, to his relief. Agios didn't dislike people, but he found himself avoiding interaction as much as possible these days—and, after all, these were Samaritans.

The stones were crumbling around the well, and a shower of dust and small pebbles trickled down and down until they plopped into the water far below. It wouldn't be cold, but it would be welcome all the same, and Agios lowered the bucket until it sank. Then hand over hand he drew it out with a heavy load of water, the weight life-giving and exhausting at once.

By the time he held the bucket, full and dripping, Agios found himself unusually weary. *What's the matter with me?* he wondered. *Getting old? Too stupid to find more shade and stay out of this blistering sun?* His pulse felt fast and fluttery, as though his heart had become too tired to pound as strongly as it should have.

He turned from the well, nearly stumbling, and gasped in the hot air. His palms felt sweaty. The short hike back to Krampus and the camel would be impossible in this state. Krampus was waiting and needed water as badly as the camel did, and Agios needed to get there as quickly as possible, but for the first time in many years he knew he had no choice but to rest. His age, his own mortality, felt as real and agonizing to him as the sun that beat down on his unprotected head.

He found a thorn tree with its flat canopy offering enough shade for him to collapse out of the sun's blaze with his back against the bark. He didn't mean to doze, but the dance of sun-spattered shadows lulled him, and his eyes fell shut. His knees were pulled up to his chest, the bucket of water tucked between his legs like a treasure far more precious than its humble vessel suggested.

How long did he sleep? Minutes? More? Agios didn't know, but when he stirred it was to the sound of a voice.

"Will you give me a drink?"

The man was dressed simply in the Hebrew fashion, a long tallit, a prayer shawl, covering his head and obscuring his face. He sat on the edge of the well, hands on his knees as if holding himself up against the sun and the exhaustion it glared down. A woman had drawn water from the well and stood staring at the man as though astonished by the request. Neither appeared to have noticed him.

Even blinking sleep from his eyes, Agios could see the shock on the woman's face. She was lovely in a dark, simple way, but her eyes filled with suspicion as she regarded the man. "You are a Jew and I a Samaritan woman. How can you ask me for a drink?"

Agios sat up straighter, sloshing water on his dusty feet and darkening the leather of his sandals. It was unheard of, a Jew asking a Samaritan for anything, especially a lone woman. Almost against his will, Agios felt a surge of sympathy for her. He saw her pride in the way she held her jaw just so, as if she was used to keeping her face set, her countenance strong so she didn't betray her true feelings. Yet Agios sensed something soft about her, as plain as the urn in her hands.

"If you knew the gift of God and who it is that asks you for a drink," the man said quietly, "you would have asked him and he would have given you living water."

The words were little louder than a whisper, but Agios heard them as surely as if they had been spoken for his benefit. The woman was already shaking her head, but something inside Agios fractured at the man's strange proclamation. His gaze shifted to the man, the thick stripes of his tallit and the tassels that lay in his lap. Who was this? What did he mean by "living water"? It sounded as foreign and magnificent as heaven itself.

Agios's head and body hurt. Every muscle ached, every joint throbbed with the months and years that he had worked and run from memories and longed for something so much more than the life he scraped together for himself and Krampus out of the hills surrounding Nazareth.

A vision came into his mind, so real—*He is doing this*, Agios thought. *Somehow he speaks to me without words and shows me my life!*

He saw it all in his mind: The ravine and the libanos trees, Philos being bitten and falling. The months of drunkenness, more of captivity. The caravans, Gamos and then Caspar. His return to gather the resin. The scent of the precious resin filled his nostrils, and it was so unexpected, so fresh and dazzling, that Agios gasped a little. And here again was Philos, his hair thick and dark as the soil where Agios planted his garden, fragrant with the smoke of burned frankincense. His golden skin glowed in the brilliance of the summer sunshine, and Agios could have wept for the beauty of it, for the way that he could taste and feel and see and almost touch the life that he had lived and the love that he had lost. Living water? Oh, God, his soul yearned for it.

The man was standing now, not much taller than the woman with whom he spoke, but with something about him that made Agios want to go and sit at his feet. His heart, which had beat so pitifully before, now filled his chest with the certainty of glory. *Something is happening, something wonderful. It will change everything.* Agios was sure of it.

She knew it, too. The woman sobbed, and though the man hadn't touched her, something about her was different. "Are you greater than our father Jacob?" she asked, wonder in her voice.

"Everyone who drinks this water will be thirsty again, but whoever drinks the water I offer will never again thirst."

Impossible! Agios sat up straighter. Surely the man was not in his right mind. But even as the thought arose, Agios dismissed it. This stranger struck him as confident, his words sincere. When he spoke, it was as if Agios were hearing truth for the very first time.

"Indeed," the man continued, "the water I give them will become in them a spring of water welling up with eternal life."

Agios put a hand to his head and felt the wrinkles around his own eyes, the deep-set lines that told the story of his many years and the road he had traveled. Eternal life? He didn't yearn for it, but something in him rose at the words, at the improbable grace of them.

Life was hard and long and heartbreaking. In a lifetime, every man eventually lost everything he loved. Who would want more of it? But contained in the agony of existence was more majesty than Agios had ever realized. He couldn't have guessed at the love that Krampus had offered him. The thought surprised him. Did Krampus love him? Yes, he did, like the father the big man had never known. And Agios loved Krampus as a friend, but even more, as a son, not Philos, but a son nonetheless.

He thought of cool mornings when mist hovered over the trees and the sun was a pink slice of ripe fig on the horizon. There was splendor in that, and in newborn lambs that were born slick and warm, already bleating. He remembered joy in the faces of the children who received Agios's humble gifts. He felt the comfort of memories that he held close, like gold hidden in the palm of his hand. All of it seemed resplendent with something grander and more profound than Agios had ever been willing to admit.

Something . . . *holy*.

It was the word that blew through Agios's heart as he watched the man at the well. And though he was not a religious man, he felt as if he was watching something consecrated, a sacrament so hallowed he felt unclean as he sat a humble witness to it.

Then Agios took the bucket in his hands and lifted the tough, leather rim to his lips. He drank deep, quenching mouthfuls that spilled down his chin and soaked his beard and tunic right through. It was ordinary water but it tasted like joy to him. Cool and satisfying on his tongue, exhilarating to his weary soul. Agios could feel himself reviving with every swallow, the strength returning to his limbs as rainwater brings new life when it douses dry ground. He felt as if he could fling aside the bucket and leap to the place where the Jewish man and the Samaritan woman stood, as if he could bound down the hill to the copse of trees where Krampus and the injured camel waited patiently for him. Agios could carry their burden to Jerusalem himself, and do it happily.

Agios would have risen and approached the unlikely pair at the well, but a small band of men had come over the rise. The woman had turned as if to go. "I know that the Messiah is coming," she said hurriedly, gathering up her empty bucket. "When he comes, he will explain everything to us."

Messiah? It had been a long time since Agios had heard

that word. But for a heartbeat or two, everything seemed clear. The man carefully pulled his tallit to his shoulders, exposing a rather ordinary face. Unremarkable features, skin the color of the dusty ground beneath their feet. His hair and beard were in need of trimming, but beneath the unruly brown curls, his deep eyes were at once sharp and kind, wise and filled with compassion. When he looked at the woman, Agios wished he were standing in her place. And just as quickly he was glad that he wasn't. To be gazed at like that? It would undo a man.

"I am he," the man said.

It was as if a cool breeze blew across the hill. Agios felt his skin prickle, his soul split open. For just a second, the man looked past the Samaritan woman, and locked eyes with Agios. The smile that crossed his lips extended to his warm eyes and beyond, but therein contained something indefinable and secret. Sadness? Agios wanted to call out, but his throat felt pinched tight.

And then the woman was gone, forgetting her pitcher. She had hiked up her skirts and run like a child, shouting as she went: "Come and see. A man who gave me a vision of everything I ever did! Could this be the Messiah?"

She had a vision, too! Messiah? Could this be?

Agios found himself standing beneath the tree, his own pail of water forgotten at his feet. It tipped and spilled its contents among the knobbed roots of the tree where Agios had received solace. It seemed a fitting offering. Yet Agios didn't know what to do. He would have stayed and stared in wonder but for one of the men who broke the spell of his trance.

"Rabbi," he said, holding out bread to the young man, "eat something."

Another added, "Please, Jesus."

Jesus.

Jesus!

King of Kings.

He has given me something—I took it in with the water I drank.

He has restored my hope.

Agios turned and ran down the hill as fast as his feet would carry him. Or rather, he flew. He was a man on fire, a man restored.

Alive.

Chapter 12

A gios's impulse was to follow Jesus, but he had re-
sponsibilities to Krampus and to the flock he owned.
Because the camel was lame, they camped for days near the
well at Sychar and sold their goods to passers-by instead
of continuing to Jerusalem. In less than a week the heavy
packs were empty, and then Agios's mind turned elsewhere. Even as he negotiated fair prices, he was making
plans. They would return to their hut near Nazareth, sell
the flock, and begin their lives as nomads.

Agios had picked up the thread of the story surrounding
Jesus in the days they waited near the well. Travelers spoke of

a prophet, a young man who practiced love for God and for all men and women. He traveled far, walking the countryside with his band of followers and preaching a gospel that few could wholly comprehend but no one could forget. People whispered of miracles they had witnessed or had heard about from trusted friends: water at a wedding feast turned into wine; a storm calmed; a leper healed instantaneously.

Agios could add his own tale to the growing narrative, but he held his tongue. What was there to say? A woman had been offered living water. Agios had drunk it. No, not literally—he had drunk earthly water, but with it he had taken in a feeling of exhilaration, and something in Agios had changed. The seed that had been planted on the night he first laid eyes on the baby beneath the star had been watered. It sprang quickly, gloriously to life, as sudden and beautiful as a desert flower.

Krampus noticed the change in his friend immediately. He didn't say anything, but Agios often caught his old friend grinning at him. It gentled the big man, and Agios couldn't help but smile back. By the surprise that lit Krampus's eyes it was obvious to Agios that he hadn't smiled enough in the years gone by. He regretted the long silences, the way he could be so remote. Krampus deserved better.

"We're going to find him," Agios told Krampus as they traveled on foot back to their hillside home.

Krampus looked at him sharply, his expression filled with disbelief and hope. "Baby Jesus?"

Agios laughed. "He's not a baby now, Krampus. He's a grown man." He almost added, "I've seen him," but it seemed an unfair admission when Krampus himself so longed for another glimpse of Jesus. The infant that Agios had carved was still, after all these years, Krampus's most prized possession.

After the sale of the camel and the sheep, Agios told Krampus that they were about to take their journey. The big man asked no questions but took his robes from a chest made of fragrant cedar wood, where for most of the time they lay carefully folded. Agios began to make a bundle of what they would need. It would be a bare minimum.

The furniture in the hut, the beds and table and chairs, he had made himself. He would leave all that. Let some poor shepherd find the hut and make a home of it. Agios did not plan to return. From as long ago as the three scholars' gift to him, and from the trades he had made as a merchant and even as a shepherd, he had a good store of coins. These he would carry in a heavy leather bag. He hesitated over his tools. True, they would add to the burden, but after all this time he felt lost without them. Every time he picked them up he remembered the miles he'd traveled, and other things: Gamos and the caravan that had plucked him off the side of the road and inadvertently saved his life. Philos. It seemed that his heart would forever return to Philos. He decided to take the tools.

Nearly three weeks had passed since Agios had witnessed Jesus and the Samaritan woman at the well, and he wasn't sure where to find the traveling prophet. Jerusalem was as good a place as any to start. That afternoon Agios and Krampus set out on foot, taking the road south. Krampus leaned heavily on a staff as they followed a dusty road that wound over low hills covered with deep green summer foliage.

At times the road rose to the summits of the hills, and then in the distance the arid, bare brown mountains loomed. Heat made them shimmer and dance. Agios was so intent on the journey that until it was time to rest, he did not notice how badly Krampus was limping. Then, concerned, he asked, "Do your knees hurt?"

Krampus nodded but did not speak. Agios realized then with a shock how old his friend was looking. He was not truly ancient—Agios had met him, when? Thirty-some years earlier. Krampus might be fifty, or close to it, but time had gnarled him into a figure even more stooped and crooked than he had been before. More crooked than Agios, who himself was well past sixty. When had he grown so old? "I'll find you an animal to ride," Agios told him.

It took another slow day of walking, but finally Agios did find a sturdy and docile little mule that was willing to bear Krampus. The big man had never sat in a saddle, and at first he lurched and clung tight to the little beast's mane and bridle, but he managed to stay in place and gradually learned to keep his balance. Still, a journey that should have taken them three days stretched out into a week.

At the magnificently arched Damascus Gate of Jerusalem, Roman guards stood watch, just as in the old days. In the heat, with only a little traffic in and out of the city, the guards were bored, and they doggedly questioned Agios: Where was he from, where was he going, and for what purpose? Agios told them, truthfully, that he had lived in the countryside for many years and added that now, growing old for his calling as a shepherd, he had come to the city seeking easier employment. He did not mention that his employment was following a prophet. Romans did not trust prophets.

"And what about him?" one of the soldiers asked, grimacing as he nodded at Krampus. "Who's this ugly fellow?"

"My son," Agios said shortly.

Krampus stared the Roman down and said, "His son."

Agios looked at him, thinking, *That's the bravest thing you've ever done.*

"Go on," the soldier said.

Throughout the city Agios found an atmosphere of fear and resentment. The Romans had tightened their grip— and they were quick to come down on anyone they suspected of plotting against them or even of thinking of doing it. At an inn, Agios overheard a merchant complaining about Jesus: "They call Jesus a holy man. What's holy about ruining our business?"

Agios sat close to him and asked a question or two. The story came out as the man drank wine, but it was spoken in hushed tones. The man was a money-changer in the Temple yard, but Jesus had passed by and had declared God's house no place for buying and selling. The man said, "He drove all us money-changers out with a whip!"

Though the man himself was Roman, Agios noticed he seemed just as wary of the authorities as the Jewish population. That afternoon he and Krampus meandered through Jerusalem, asking about this prophet. Many were too afraid to speak at all. Others would only whisper a few words: Jesus had been baptized by John, and then not long ago Herod had John executed. Herod Antipas, a woman explained, son of Herod the Great and ruler of Galilee. "At least he doesn't hold power here," she said. "The Roman procurator Pilate governs Judea."

From what others said, Agios gathered that Jesus was no longer in Jerusalem, nor was he likely to return soon. Where was he, then? Out in the countryside, traveling from place to place, spreading his message. Agios needed a clue—where had Jesus traveled, and in what direction could Agios search for him?

Finally, he found a man who knew about Jesus of Nazareth and was able to help them pick up the trail. "I've been following him for weeks," the stranger said in a reverent voice. "He is a holy man."

"How do you know?" Agios asked.

"By his deeds." The stranger spoke of miraculous cures— people who came to Jesus blind and went away able to see again, and a madman whose spirit grew calm and peaceful at a word from Jesus, and most of all, a child healed of some mysterious illness.

"She was dead," the man whispered. "Yet at a word from him, she recovered and lives still."

"Where is Jesus now?" Agios asked.

"He was in Jericho two weeks ago," the man said. "And then meant to go to Galilee from what I understand."

That very evening, Agios and Krampus left Jerusalem the same way they had entered it.

"We go home now?" Krampus muttered, confused.

"Do you want to go back to Nazareth, son?" Agios asked him gently. Their journey was a lot to ask of a man who so clearly struggled along the way. Krampus never complained, but though Agios did not want to settle down again, he worried about his adopted son. Jesus of Nazareth—and Egypt and Bethlehem and everywhere and nowhere, it seemed—was an inexorable pull. Agios had spent more than thirty years searching for something to soothe his broken soul, and he had been given a taste of the peace he craved. He wanted more.

If Jesus would allow it, Agios would follow him until the very end of his days. And if he wouldn't, Agios had already decided to follow anyway, as he had decades earlier, a protector at a distance, willing to defend Jesus to the death. Still, all of that was much to ask of Krampus. "Do you want to go home?" Agios repeated reluctantly.

"No," Krampus said firmly. "We go find Jesus."

Agios thought, *Our mission has always been to follow him— but at a distance! Not to put him in danger*. Still, for the first time in decades, Agios felt as if he could understand Krampus's obsession with the baby and then the boy. Krampus needed to see Jesus for himself, and they were in this together.

Agios put his hand on Krampus's chest, over the place where his heart thumped its irregular beat. "Then we will find him," he said. And suddenly, the other reason he longed to see Jesus again slipped off his tongue before he could hold it back. "We'll find him and he'll heal you, my son."

A smile tugged at the corner of Krampus's mouth. He gave his head a little shake.

"You don't want to be healed?" Agios asked.

Krampus thought for a moment, his brows drawing together as he tried to summon the right words. It was obvious that he wanted to say something important, and that whatever it was weighed heavily on him. But in the end, he couldn't conjure more than the simplest statement: "Father, I don't need healing."

Agios didn't understand.

They traveled up to Ephraim and through Samaria, always a step behind Jesus. However, he left evidence of his passage in his wake. Some grateful people had been healed, other dissatisfied folks had heard his message and felt confused and troubled by it—and some were even angry, claiming that Jesus would bring the anger of the Romans down on them all. However, most spoke of wonder, amazement, and awe. A wind was beginning to blow across the land, whispering of change and hope and rest for weary souls. To Agios, it also carried with it the scent of an impending storm.

The subtle shift in the atmosphere made him uneasy.

Krampus was no longer a hardy traveler and required many stops. Because there were more than enough coins in the leather pouch that Agios carried, and even more hidden inside his cloak—concealed in the same manner that he had once carried nuggets of frankincense—they stayed at inns nearly every night. Krampus was so weary he even agreed to sleep upon a bed. He acted as if the stale straw covered with musty blankets to make a rough mattress was fit for a king, and as if he was woefully undeserving of such comfort.

As the days passed, Agios felt as if time was slipping through his fingers, the sands of an hourglass spilling so quickly there was nothing he could do to restrain it. They journeyed through Capernaum, Tyre, and Caesarea Phillipi, and when Bethsaida was behind them Krampus suddenly slumped over the neck of his plodding gray mule. Agios had been walking with his hand on the animal's halter and he caught his old friend almost by accident. The mule, sensing something was amiss, stopped and let Agios pull Krampus from his bowed back.

"You are not too heavy for me these days," Agios said lightly as he lowered Krampus to the ground. His friend's breath was coming high and fast in his chest, his palms slick with sudden sweat. "Do you need a drink?"

Krampus didn't respond. His entire body was taut, strung tight in the grip of his unpredictable heart. It was racing again; Agios knew it without even checking. He was all too familiar with the way Krampus's lips would slowly turn blue, his arms stiffen and bend until they were curved toward his body like bowstrings overstretched and fit to snap. If Agios put his ear to Krampus's chest, he would not be able to make out the beats or even attempt to count them. They would rush together, a herd of horses galloping so fast the whir of it left him dizzy.

There was nothing Agios could do. He sat beside his ungainly adopted son, and while Krampus's closed eyelids fluttered, Agios told him stories.

He spun tales of the caravan and their first days together, how Krampus made Gamos laugh with the unusual sounds he could make, and of Caspar's kindness and Melchior's grand home in Megisthes. He reminded Krampus of the starry nights and fever-hot days, the meals they had shared and the moments of contentment. He also spoke of the fisher boys at the beach in Egypt and the first time they experienced one of Krampus's episodes together. He said they'd never been far from Jesus in all that time.

"We'll find him, now," Agios told Krampus. "And when we do, he'll heal you."

Krampus moaned.

"We won't leave him again. I promise."

The attack passed gradually, but by the time Krampus

could sit up it was too late to journey on. Agios set up a makeshift camp for them along the side of the road, and they spent the night under the stars just like they had in the old days.

That night, Krampus murmured, "I am your son. You said."

"You are not really, but I'm proud to call you that. I hope I've been the father you never knew," Agios told him.

"Father. If I die, promise me?"

Agios tried to sound cheerful: "You're not going to die. They say Jesus can even conquer death. He'll help you, you'll see."

"Yes. But promise, father?" Krampus insisted.

"What?"

"Bury me in water," Krampus said. "My mother say once, your father buried in ocean. Maybe in water I find him. Then even away from you, I still have a father. Bury me in water."

"I promise, son," Agios said. "But you'll live a long time yet." Krampus smiled and fell asleep.

It seemed divine that when they woke the following morning it was to news of Jesus.

"Have you two come to seek him? He's here!" a man said

as he hurried by the place where Agios and Krampus ate a simple meal of barley bread and dates.

"Where?" Agios was already on his feet, calling after the man. He didn't even need to ask who the man was referring to—only Jesus could engender that sort of response in people.

"By the Sea of Galilee! They say he will preach to the crowd!"

Agios struck camp quickly, rolling their mats and tying them to the mule so haphazardly that Krampus laughed.

"You think I'm funny?" Agios grinned, helping his friend to stand. "Laugh all you want, Krampus. Today we see Jesus!" And then, Agios pulled Krampus to him and embraced the man he loved as a son. It was an uncharacteristic move, something that Agios hadn't done in years. When was the last time he had touched another person in this way? He couldn't recall even a moment of such physical affection in the last decade—two? three?—and all at once he stung with regret.

Yet Krampus clung to him, fists bunching the fabric of Agios's cloak and head bent to his shoulder. They stood like that for a long time, holding each other, until Agios pulled away abruptly. His eyes felt hot, his throat thick and aching.

"Friend," Krampus said, and reached out to put his hand on Agios's head. "Father."

"Yes," Agios smiled. "I am your friend, Krampus. And your father."

They set off, Krampus on the mule and Agios leading the animal, hurrying as fast as he dared. The hills around the Sea of Galilee obscured their view until they crested a low rise and saw a great crowd spread out before them. The bowl of a small valley opened toward the lake, the blue water bright and sparkling in the morning sun. And all throughout a field of dry, brown grasses, people of every size and age and shape and color were gathered.

"There must be thousands," Agios whispered, and felt his hope dim. How would they ever find Jesus in the midst of such a throng?

But Krampus was grinning. "See him! Look there!"

Agios opened his mouth to ask where, but people thronged around them, mothers holding their children's hands and men running sure-footed. "The teacher is going to speak," one woman told her companion as she rushed by.

"Where is he?" Agios called.

She glanced back for just a moment. "On the hill. Come quickly."

Agios pulled the mule along, Krampus swaying on his back, until they were at the very outskirts of the assembly. It would be impossible to cut through the crowd, especially with the lumbering mule. Agios felt disappointment choking him. They would never see Jesus in this mass, let alone get close enough to see him, touch him, or speak to him. But Krampus didn't seem to mind. He was already slipping off the back of the mule and settling himself in the brittle grass.

"We won't be able to hear him from this far away," Agios said, trying not to sound bitter.

"Sit," Krampus told him.

So Agios sat, and strained to see past the heads of so many people before him. There, up on the hill, a man stood alone. The same white robes. The same striped tallit. Agios's eyes were not as good as they once were, yet he knew that it was Jesus. If only they could approach, if Agios could only ask Jesus to heal his friend—

It was a wish almost too precious to hold.

"We're too far away." Agios could have wept for the injustice of it.

"Shhh." Krampus waved his hand.

And then Jesus began to speak.

It seemed impossible that they could hear him clearly, but the breeze that made the grasses dance conspired with the basin of the valley between the high, rocky hills and carried Jesus's every word to them. Agios was so surprised he missed the first few things Jesus said. Jesus spoke with certainty—he obviously knew that here the earth had created something like a Roman amphitheater, where his words traveled distinct and far. Agios could sense the crowd holding its collective breath as they hung on every word, and he turned his attention to the Teacher.

"Blessed are the poor in spirit, for theirs is the kingdom of heaven."

Blessed?

Agios could not have heard him properly. This was not the order of things. Everyone knew it.

"Blessed are the mourners, for they will be comforted. Blessed are the meek, for they will inherit the earth. Blessed are those who hunger and thirst after righteousness, for they will be filled . . ."

Blessed. Blessed. Blessed—nonsense!

Agios clenched his fists, clamped his jaw so tight it began to throb. How could Jesus say such things? The poor in spirit were not blessed, nor the mourners and the meek and the hungry and thirsty. There was no good fortune in this, nothing beautiful or happy or consecrated. Agios knew this with every ounce of his being.

He had lived a life poor in spirit, a life of mourning, he had hungered and thirsted for peace and righteousness. Krampus had become the meekest of men. Such things were curses, not blessings. He was cursed. Krampus was cursed.

But when Agios looked at his friend, he saw tears were streaming down Krampus's cheeks. Love shone in his eyes, and in his expression Agios saw the peace that he himself had spent the better part of his life seeking.

It was as if scales fell from his eyes.

In that moment, Agios saw Krampus clearly for the first time. His friend, his brother, was a man of twisted body but of pure heart. *What must life be like for him? A world achingly complicated, and yet childishly simple. Krampus can forgive all the world has done to him and can accept the pain that has been and that will come again—and he can still find joy in the words he hears. He has the faith of a child.*

I have not, Agios admitted bitterly.

And yet, though he had mourned for a lifetime, had he not found comfort in caring for Krampus? Krampus was not Philos, yet he had grown to love Agios unselfishly. In small ways the big man did all he could—trying to cook for Agios, taking his watches to let Agios sleep, carrying out Agios's requests, taking tender care of the goats and the sheep. *He has lived a life of love and service. I have tried to cut myself off from love because—because love can pierce like a knife. Was I wrong?*

He had fought a hard world with drink. He had served Caspar with resentment at first and then with a weary willingness. He had put up with Krampus at first because Krampus was of all men more miserable than he. Agios had been seeking a way to find joy again, to live again.

And Jesus offered it.

It was so unexpected, so difficult to fathom, to grasp and believe, that Agios couldn't quite get his heart all the way around it. But everything Jesus was saying was true—and his soul knew it long before his mind could accept it.

Agios's poor spirit had been given a kingdom of incredible riches: health and friendship and work for his hands. Agios had kept counsel with kings and slaves. He had witnessed the coming of the Messiah himself. He had known deep and lasting love. And meek Krampus, who had experienced such sorrow, sat reverent at the foot of the hill, looking up as if the kingdom of God were coming.

No, as if it were already here.

When Agios's soul was thirsty, hadn't Jesus himself given him water to drink?

Not from the well, no. But the living water he had spoken of.

Unthinkable grace.

Without looking, Krampus reached out and took Agios's hand. They sat, two old men, brothers, their bent and gnarled fingers holding tight as they listened. As they learned.

God, Agios silently prayed, *lift this burden from me. Take my hatred and guilt, take my anger and sorrow and blame. I don't deserve your help—I know that. I let my own son die from my arrogance and my pride, from my belief that I could protect him. But even if I'm without hope forever, though, please do this for me. Do it, and I will protect and serve Jesus until his mission is complete.*

The hot tears had come. *Heal Krampus. I'm just a broken old man and there's nothing you can do for me, but make him whole.*

And on the mount, Jesus's words continued as he spoke

of giving alms to the poor: "give your alms to the poor secretly," he said, "and thy Father which seeth in secret himself shall reward thee openly."

Help him. Please. Help my son.

For a long time after Jesus had ceased speaking and had gone, Agios and Krampus remained sitting there, still as the crowd thronged around them. Some had gone toward Jesus, and Agios felt a desire to follow them—and yet he had sworn to protect Jesus from a distance.

He studied Krampus and saw him as though for the first time. The surface didn't matter anymore, not his twisted limbs or his misshapen face. Agios saw the purity of his soul, the serene surrender of his spirit to something greater than all of mankind.

Closing his eyes, Agios murmured, "I will follow the Messiah. Grant that I may be a grateful servant to him. Let me serve him until his mission is completed."

He gasped. For a moment he had felt filled with light—the same light he had seen in a vision, the same light that the star had shone down over Bethlehem.

Agios opened his eyes again and saw Krampus smiling at him—and the light faded.

But it was there! It was within me! I felt it!

Agios breathed deeply, and he sensed that somehow someone was answering his prayer: *Surely a man who can raise the dead can heal my son. It can't be dangerous for him if we can just get close enough to ask, to beg, for healing.*

He got to his feet and said to Krampus, "Come. We have something to do."

Chapter 13

✦

From that day, Agios and Krampus followed Jesus like a shadow. Sometimes the distance between them stretched as long as a dark silhouette cast by a setting sun. These were the times when Krampus was ailing or too weak to ride the mule. Often they would lose the trail and have to pick it up again by questioning townspeople and travelers. But as Jesus's reputation grew, it became easier to discover where he had been and where he might be going next. All the same, Agios hated being a step behind. Not everyone loved Jesus the way he and Krampus did.

Other times they were able to keep pace, or ended up stumbling into a village or city at almost the same glorious moment that Jesus and his followers did. The crowds were growing larger, and it became all but impossible to get close to him. In one town, the throng of people was so thick a group of men carried their paralyzed friend to the roof of the house where Jesus was teaching and lowered him through the tiles. Not much later, Krampus laughed to see the crippled man dance through the crowd, the name of God on his lips and his frail, twisted legs healthy and strong.

Agios would have done the same, would have slung Krampus over his back and dropped him through the roof if it meant that Jesus might whisper healing over his broken body, but the crowd erupted before he had the chance. Some followed the healed paralytic, joining in his dance of worship. Others whispered that the Rabbi's offering forgiveness for sins was blasphemy from the lips of a mere man, a man who claimed he was God. A group of scribes and Pharisees pushed through the masses, and by the set of their bleak faces Agios knew that Jesus had made as many enemies as friends.

Wherever Jesus went, controversy followed.

"He's a revolutionary," Agios told Krampus later that night. "He's going to change things. I just don't know how."

"Jesus, you mean," Krampus said softly, the word a blessing, an incantation. "Jesus."

Agios knew Krampus was slipping a little every day, failing slowly. He would die soon. Agios was sure of it. And although he knew that death was the end of everyone's journey, that it was a fate none could escape, he couldn't stand the thought of it happening *now*. Not yet. Not when Jesus might heal him.

The peace that Agios had spent so much of his life pursuing, the forgiveness, and the blessed assurance that all was well and would be well, shimmered on the horizon. He could see it glowing there, beckoning him.

If only Jesus could heal Krampus's body and Agios's spirit. If only they could be with him. If only.

Agios took to praying during the nights when he couldn't sleep and Krampus breathed slow and shallow. He didn't really know how to pray, but Jesus had taught his followers and they passed the words as carefully as the most fragile of treasures. "Our Father, who art in heaven, hallowed be Thy name . . ."

Often Agios kept going, talking to God as if he were a friend in the room instead of an unknown entity that he couldn't see or touch or hear. It was comforting, even though he still knew little about the Hebrew God and was probably going about it all wrong. He knew priests had lists of rules and regulations, things he should and shouldn't do. Still, he knew what he wanted, and as the months passed and the two old men continued their pilgrimage, Agios found himself repeating the very same imperative night after night. It was his creed, his most heartfelt supplication—a longing that began to equal even his desire for healing: *Let me serve him.*

Agios wasn't entirely sure how he would serve Jesus, but was confident that if he could find a way to approach Jesus without putting him in danger, if he finally had the chance to see Jesus face-to-face, everything would become clear.

On a morning during the Hebrew Passover season, Agios and Krampus again approached the gates of Jerusalem. The dawn was cool, the air damp and gray. Normally, the unlikely pair would be following in the footsteps of

Jesus, strangers in towns they would never again visit. However, Agios knew that Jesus would be in Jerusalem for Passover, and they had made their way toward the city with all the speed that Agios could muster and Krampus could stand. Still, they were late.

Now ahead of them, against the gradually lightening eastern sky, the crenellated walls of Jerusalem stood black, the orange-red glow of torches marking the Zion Gate. Agios led the mule by its halter, and for the last two hours it had plodded along quietly. On its back Krampus slumped, breathing heavily, asleep in the saddle. He had at least learned enough balance not to fall.

Something in the air seemed expectant, reminding Agios of the prophecy in the star, the brilliant light that had led them to Bethlehem all those years ago—but instead of radiance and glory, the warm luster of hope, he felt somehow the earth growing solemn, darker. The sun should have been up by now, not lost in mists. It felt to Agios like the world was dragging its feet, loath to begin a day that buzzed heavy with malevolence.

Jesus. It had to be. Who else could cause the heavens themselves to slow? Agios had heard rumors of a storm on the Sea of Galilee, of the way Jesus stilled the tempest, of how he could command even the wind and the waves. What was happening now?

On the road just ahead of them walked two dozen or more travelers, probably Jewish pilgrims journeying to Jerusalem for Passover. Agios hurried the mule along until he joined a few stragglers near the rear of the group. Up toward the gate one of the older men spoke with the guards, who said something and then sent them through and into the city.

Whispers ran back through the crowd, and they reached Agios's ears: "Trouble in Jerusalem. The Sanhedrin have tried a Jewish man for blasphemy, for threatening to destroy the Temple. They say they'll execute him."

Agios felt his heart go cold. *Blasphemy*. How often had he heard that word associated with Jesus? He swallowed against the tightness in his throat and gripped the mule's reins tighter.

One of the two elders walking near Agios said firmly, "The Sanhedrin don't have the power of life and death—the Romans won't allow that. The Romans themselves will have to confirm any judgment of a Jewish court. This man will have to appear before Pilate for judgment."

Agios pushed forward, his skin prickling in apprehension, and grabbed the speaker's sleeve. The man—his clothing and his long gray beard showed him to be a rabbi—looked at him in surprise. "Where will he be?" Agios asked. "This man you speak of, who has been accused of rebellion. Where will Pilate try him?"

The rabbi stroked his beard and stared at him in the pallid half-light of dawn. He said with a frown, "Friend, why do you want to know such things? You're not Jewish."

"I'm interested in what happens to him," Agios replied impatiently. He repeated, "Where will Pilate try him?"

A woman spoke up. "I can tell you. Pilate always holds court north of the temple, usually in the courtyard of the fortress. You may be able to get in to see. Roman trials are public, unless it's a question of a plot against the emperor."

Though the sun was still low and dimly red in the waxen sky, already masses of people filled the streets of Jerusalem. They surged in a mixture of scents, animal and human sweat, the dung of horses and mules, the aromas of cooked foods. Agios never liked the smell of cities. It was too much like the stench of despair.

As Agios and Krampus pushed through the press of the crowds, he overheard bits and pieces: "The Sanhedrin said he threatened to destroy the temple . . . Pilate is questioning him in public . . . one of his followers denied even knowing him . . ." The mood of the place grew dark with conflicting emotions: anger and resentment and fear and foreboding.

They tried to make their way north, but the broadest streets were the ones most choked with foot traffic, and when they found their passage blocked for a moment and had to turn down an alley to find an alternate way, Krampus put a big hand on Agios's shoulder. He patted Agios's upper arm, his awkward way of trying to offer comfort. It was meant to be reassuring, but Krampus himself looked frightened and sick.

Agios nodded but did not trust himself to speak. *Now*, he thought or prayed, beseeching the heavens. *Do it now. In this heavy hour, reveal that he is King of Kings.* Jesus had cast out demons, healed lepers, and raised people from the dead. Surely the rebellion he was inciting, the revolution that would turn the whole world upside down, was happening now.

"Have faith," Agios whispered, and didn't realize he had said it out loud until Krampus echoed him: "Faith."

Still, Agios's heart hammered painfully in his chest, and his mind raced with worry. He and Krampus threaded their way through the crowds and followed the street as it climbed the Temple Mount. It was only a few hundred steps now to the fortress. The gates stood open, and the crush of people stood thickest just outside. The courtyard was full to bursting already.

Agios tried to find a way through to the fortress gate, and the two of them made slow progress, but near the gateway courtyard they met an impassable flood of people pouring out and coming the other way. Agios stopped one of them, a poorly dressed man whose expression looked desolate. "What has happened?" Agios asked him. "Is it . . ." He could hardly bring himself to say the name, he was so afraid of the answer. "Jesus?"

The man looked frightened, but he tugged Agios into the shelter of a deep, shaded doorway and then as the yelling crowd surged past he leaned in close and said softly, "Yes." It confirmed what Agios already knew, but he felt his heart pitch just the same. "Pilate asked Jesus if he claimed to be king of the Jews, but Jesus wouldn't answer one way or the other. Pilate declares that he can't find evidence to support the charges the Sanhedrin raised. He can find no harm in Jesus."

Agios sagged with relief. "Pilate didn't judge him? Then he's been released? He's free?"

The man gulped a deep breath and replied, "No. Jesus told Pilate that he was from Galilee. Pilate decided that since he came here from Herod Antipas's realm, Herod has the proper jurisdiction and must judge him. He sent Jesus to Herod for trial."

Agios suppressed a moan. "To Tiberias in Perea?"

"No, not Herod's capital," the man replied, a little impatiently. "Herod is here in the city. He came for Passover."

The man started to move from the doorway, but Agios stopped him, gripping his arm above the elbow. "Please. Tell me, where can I find Herod?"

"I don't know. I—I'm not of Jerusalem, I'm not even Jewish. I came here following—" The man darted a glance around. The crowd was thinning, everyone heading southward now, and no one seemed to notice them. Still, the man whispered, "Are you one of us? A follower of Jesus?"

The air seemed to go unnaturally still and Agios stifled a shiver. The man's fear was like an infectious disease. Suddenly, the man took a few steps back, glancing around as if he wished he had never dared to ask the question at all. He almost fled into the street.

Agios also went back into the crowd, Krampus limping at his side. People jostled and shoved at them, but Agios did not react. That morning the streets of Jerusalem seemed like channels carved by waves on a stony shore of the sea, ebbing and flowing with a tide of agitated people. Some of them knew more than others, and Agios questioned a good many.

By the time Agios and Krampus reached the place where Herod was said to be staying, they were too late. From people in the crowd they learned that Herod, too, had briefly questioned Jesus before sending him back to Pilate. Agios felt trapped in a nightmare, snared in a fever-dream that at turns chilled him and set his blood ablaze. He stumbled through the street with Krampus clinging to his sleeve and felt each word like an assault.

"Herod commanded Jesus to perform magic for him, do some miracles, but Jesus stood silent."

"He accused Jesus of being a follower of John the Baptist . . ."

"They dressed him in a robe befitting the king of the Jews, and sent him back again to Pilate."

The sun had climbed high enough to show above the city walls and cast its sickly light on the eastern side of the Temple. Because of the throngs of people, Agios and Krampus took a long, indirect way around, but still they could not force their way into the square courtyard where Pilate sat in judgment. "What's happening?" Agios asked, and it seemed at first that no one knew.

Finally, though, a man who had climbed to a window ledge opposite the gate where he could look over the heads of the crowd called down, "Pilate asks: 'Do you want me to release to you the king of the Jews or the rebel Barabbas?' He wants to spare Jesus! Barabbas is a thief, a murderer some say, a revolutionary—"

From the front, from the middle, from everywhere Agios turned, the cry rose: "Barabbas!"

Agios knew it was customary for the Roman governor to release a prisoner of the crowd's choice during the Passover festival. But a notorious criminal instead of Jesus? What were they doing?

"Give us Barabbas!" The sound echoed in the streets around the fortress. The crowd was getting out of hand. Agios could feel the hostile shift and watched, horrified, as men began to clench their fists and raise them heavenward. "Give us Barabbas!"

And, then, just as quickly as the outcry began, the crowd hushed in a sweeping wave. A moment of near silence, the earth held its breath, and Agios could just make out the words. He didn't know if they came from Pilate himself or if they were broadcast by the man on the ledge, but they filled him with dread all the same.

"What shall I do, then, with the one you call the king of the Jews?"

The shout was vicious. Instantaneous. It was as if the crowd had been waiting for this moment, as if an insane brew of hatred had been fermenting for years. Decades. Longer. And maybe it had been.

"Crucify him!"

Krampus looked as if he were moaning, but Agios couldn't hear him over the tumult. The shouts were wildfire roaring through the crowd, consuming it. "Crucify him! Crucify him! Crucify him!" Krampus collapsed, his grip tearing Agios's sleeve. The violence of the masses, the bloodlust for a man whom Agios only knew as a boundless source of love and hope and peace, terrified Agios, and he saw his own fear reflected in the eyes of his friend. He pulled Krampus to his feet before the crowd could trample him.

As Agios half-carried and half-pulled Krampus, he saw one old man rip his tunic in a Hebrew gesture of deep mourning. Others shoved at the graybeard, jeering and laughing. His face streamed with tears as they tore his clothes further, as they spat on him.

They turn from peace and want blood instead. Madness. Like a disease, madness consumes them!

Agios managed to drag himself and Krampus through the furious press of people and slip down a relatively secluded side street. The throb and beat of the crowd was only minimally lessened here, and Agios found he had to cup Krampus's face and shout into his ear to be heard.

"I must find him!" he cried, his voice breaking. "He needs me!" His own prayer, his promise, echoed in the hollow cavern of his chest. *Let me serve him until his mission is completed.* Jesus's mission couldn't be over yet. *Not yet.*

Krampus's hands found Agios's hair and he pulled his old friend's forehead to his own. "I go with you, Father," Krampus said in a harsh voice that would not stand for a refusal, and with those words he was the brute Agios had first known, fierce and loyal and strong. There was no mistaking his meaning. Agios was ready to abandon Krampus, to leave him somewhere safe so that he could fulfill the covenant he made without putting his friend in harm's way. But Krampus was right.

They were in this together.

"We will find him," Agios said, and was shocked to taste salt. There were tears on his cheeks, his lips, in his beard. Were they his or Krampus's? Did it matter? "We'll find him together. Come, son."

They set out through the city, the howl of the crowd still ringing in their ears.

Crucify him.

Chapter 14

Crucifixion was the Romans' cruelest punishment: they drove spikes through wrists and heels and raised the victims up, their bodies bent and sagging, their chests arching hopelessly toward life as they slowly suffocated. Anguish, exhaustion, and finally the body's slow betrayal brought on a death that the victim in the end yearned for. As punishment it was unnatural, it was wrong. It was evil.

Agios panted as he hurried through the streets, Krampus's arm thrown over his shoulders for support. He felt winded, but more, sick with panic. He would have vomited if he'd had anything in his stomach to reject, but his belly was cold and empty, as hollow as his aching heart. He trudged on.

They are going to crucify him.

It was difficult even to think it, impossible to accept. Surely someone would realize what was happening. Surely Pilate would come to his senses and understand that this could not be done. But they said Pilate had called for a basin of water and, in the presence of all who were gathered there, washed his hands of the entire affair. Of Jesus.

Impossible.

Now, Agios prayed, directing his entreaty heavenward. *Do it now. If you are who Caspar believes you are—and Melchior and Balthasar and Krampus—show your power now! Revolution, a new order, a new kingdom. Bring it now!*

But even as he wished it so, a part of Agios already knew that Jesus would not stop this. The man who caressed a child's soft curls, taught forgiveness and love for neighbor and peace—would he take up a sword and fight? Would he shout a battle cry, bloody his own hands, end the lives of the very people who filled his eyes with a compassion that Agios still couldn't grasp? Never.

It's up to me, Agios thought. But he was chained to Krampus, weighted by his old friend's bulk against his own aging frame. And he'd come unarmed. Their provisions were with the mule in the stable where they had quickly tethered their animal upon entering Jerusalem. For all Agios knew, some thief had stolen them. Not that it mattered. Not that anything mattered with Jesus being nailed to a cross.

A crowd streamed north out of the city gates on the road to Golgotha, the place of the skull, and whispers drifted through the people like mist. People spoke of a crown of thorns, a scarlet robe, and the vicious bite of a Roman whip.

Krampus moaned and wept at that. Even after all these years, he carried the memory of a Roman scourge as clearly as he carried the crisscrossed scars on his back.

"I'm coming," Agios muttered through clenched teeth, tears of rage and grief flowing hot on his cheeks. Krampus gave him a look filled with sorrow and confusion, and Agios bit his tongue.

I won't give up hope! I swore to protect Jesus! I swore it to God!

They followed the multitude, caught up in the wave of humanity. From time to time Agios would try to press forward, through the mob, to drag Krampus along with him so that they could make better time on the path to the domed, rocky hill where the crucifixions were to take place. But the sea of people and the burden around his neck prevented him. He could have screamed at the injustice of it and wept for the guilt and despair it churned up in his soul.

By the time they made it to Golgotha, Agios was staggering, and Krampus—though decidedly weaker—was trying to support him. Agios felt half blind, unable to see clearly. A dense fog had risen around him, brought on by terror and disbelief. What if he couldn't fulfill his promise? What if it was already too late? He looked at Krampus and croaked, "Philos, why doesn't he free himself?"

Krampus gave him a sideways glance. "Philos?"

Not Philos. Why did I say Philos? With an effort, Agios focused his eyes and his mind. "Krampus," he murmured. "Krampus."

His friend pulled him forward. "Come. I help."

He can barely walk, and he's supporting me. I'm failing him! Failing Krampus, failing Jesus!

In the distance the execution party had climbed to the top of the hill. The Romans had prepared everything, working with their usual lethal efficiency. Within a few moments a cross rose, then another to its left and a third to its right. Men had been nailed to all three. Agios wiped his eyes and led Krampus to a place where they could stand on a boulder.

Agios's heart felt as though it would burst. At the foot of the center cross knelt a woman whom he could recognize even at a distance. She was older and bent, but the humble slant of her head and the curve of her lovely profile were burned in his mind.

Mary.

"It's Jesus. It's really him." Agios's voice cracked around a sob. He had hoped for a different outcome, for a last-minute reprieve, anything. He clenched his fists, ready in his anger to fling himself off the boulder and fight his way to the cross. He would—what? Defeat them all, help Jesus down? One man?

Krampus made a sound in the back of his throat and Agios turned his attention to his immediate surroundings. Ranks of Roman soldiers hemmed in the crowd. Some of them walked through, dispersing groups, shoving men and menacing them with spears and swords. *The tyrants truly fear rebellion*, Agios thought. As the soldiers pushed back, lashing out at people who moved too slowly, Krampus drew his turban lower on his head. He looked down at the earth and whimpered like a beaten dog, like a child whose heart had been broken.

Yet Agios couldn't comfort his friend, not now, not at this moment. *I allowed myself to hope—for the first time since I lost my son, I allowed myself to hope!* And, then, he admitted something even more painful: *I saw him for myself. I* believed.

Agios climbed down from the rock and took Krampus by the arm. Without a word he pushed his way through the crowd, desperate to get closer to Jesus, to look in his eyes and see what was written there. If Jesus so much as nodded, Agios would explode. He was still strong, his body muscled. His favorite carving knife was in his belt. It wasn't a weapon, but it would suffice.

When only a handful of men stood between them and the cross where Jesus hung, Agios found he couldn't take another step. He wanted to raise his eyes and finally see the Teacher face-to-face, but his heart was as heavy as a millstone in his chest, his feet rooted to the ground. Krampus wept silently, and as Agios stared at the trampled earth he realized that the soldiers were dividing up Jesus's clothes by casting lots.

They can't do this. He is the Messiah! Agios thought. *He knew, he knew with all his soul. Jesus is the only one who can heal my son Krampus! Only he! It's my duty to protect Jesus in exchange for his healing! I know! I know! He is the Messiah, he is!*

Then, as if something evil were slyly whispering in his ear, came the thought *Is he? Is he, really?*

So much in Agios's life had been a lie—the belief that he could protect Weala and his children, the thought that wine would ease sorrow, the idea that frankincense would bring wealth and ease to his family. *Don't let this be a lie, too! Let this man Jesus truly be the Messiah! Let him work a miracle now—*

Then from the centermost cross came the voice Agios had grown to love: "Father, forgive them, for they do not know what they are doing."

Agios caught his breath. *Hung in agony, on a tree, and still on his mission!* It couldn't end with the Messiah nailed to a cross, hanging on a tree—his own son dead on a tree—Agios pushed forward. "Rabbi!" he called, and a Roman soldier thrust a menacing sword at him. It caught him on the face, just missing his left eye, and he fell back.

"Father!" Krampus said, catching him.

Furious, Agios shook his head, blood dripping. The

slash started at the bridge of his nose and cut diagonally across his left cheek. He ripped a piece of his sleeve off and pressed it to the wound. Reached for his carving knife—

Krampus caught his arm, and he looked into the big man's eyes. "Forgive," Krampus mouthed without speaking aloud. "Not evil for evil."

The anger left Agios. Jesus had looked into the eyes of the lowest sinners—the prostitute and the tax collector and even the demon-possessed—and had spoken love and forgiveness to them. And now Krampus, the most down-trodden of them all, spoke the same message.

Still, Agios believed there must be an end point to grace, a line that even such love and forgiveness would not, could not cross.

For love was all too simple, too idealistic and self-less and pure. The world was a dark and desperate place. Surely there was room in Jesus's kingdom for death by the sword—an eye for an eye and a tooth for a tooth. Every man for himself and my people, my interests, my life above all others.

And yet Jesus looked with compassion on the very people who were killing him. He pleaded with the Father on their behalf, begging for the forgiveness of a sin that eclipsed them all. It defied everything.

In this kingdom, more violence would accomplish nothing.

Agios could hardly stand it. He had blood on his own hands, and though spilling it had felt necessary at the time—right, even—he was ashamed of his deeds in the presence of Jesus. The Teacher was silent even unto death.

Forgive me! he wanted to cry.

But Jesus wasn't looking at Agios. He was talking to the man who hung beside him.

The criminal groaned, "Remember me when you come into your kingdom."

Jesus answered him, "Truly I tell you, today you will be with me in paradise."

Paradise.

Agios couldn't bear another moment. He slid his arm around Krampus's waist and hauled his old friend through the people. The crowd parted for them, some sensing Agios's utter despair, some probably frightened of the deformed man.

"Stay!" Krampus begged. "Stay! Jesus is here!"

But Agios couldn't stay. His world was crumbling. Even the earth seemed to acknowledge the perversion of it all. The clouds that had threatened all day finally swallowed up the sun and it became so dark it was as if night had fallen hours early.

Chaos.

Darkness.

Agios and Krampus stumbled through streets awash in weeping and savagery and rumors. The temple veil was torn. Jesus was a madman. He was a righteous man.

He was the Son of God.

The earth shook, the rocks split, and even tombs broke open.

And in an abandoned side street, Agios and Krampus sat slumped against a wall and held on to each other as the world revolted. Jesus was an insurrectionist, but it was the earth itself that rebelled.

When it was over, Krampus lifted his head and swept a fine dusting of soot and stones from his brow. "It is finished," he said, his voice breaking on the word.

It was finished, Agios was sure of that. Jesus was dead, and with him all the hope that was left in the world. *A lie. A lie! I served a lie!*

"Come, son," Agios croaked, stumbling to his feet. They had to get out of Jerusalem. They had to leave. Now. He doubted his own sanity could survive much longer in this place of death, destruction, and madness.

Agios didn't realize that Krampus wasn't following him until he was several strides down the empty street. When he missed his friend, he spun on his heel to command Krampus to come instead of lingering buried in his own sadness. They were strong men, and beneath his sorrow Agios was beginning to feel the bitter burn of anger.

But Krampus wasn't crying anymore. He slumped against the stone wall and was staring after Agios with a faraway look in his eye. Agios knew that look all too well.

Hurrying back, he fell to his knees and cradled Krampus's head in his hands. It was too much: the entire experience had been far too much for Krampus to take, and he was paying for it now. It had been mere minutes, but already Krampus's cheeks were ghostly, gray. His lips parted as he wheezed.

"This will pass," Agios assured him, but a seed of panic had been planted in his heart. "This will pass and we'll go back to our hills. I'll buy more sheep. We'll never speak of Jesus again."

Krampus tried to sit up straighter. "No," he said. "No . . ."

Agios put his hands on Krampus's shoulders and pushed him down. "Rest," he cautioned. "Don't try to move."

But Krampus ignored him. He patted his garments, fumbling around as he writhed in desperation.

Agios burst out: "What! What do you want?"

Krampus lifted his hand. In his palm was the little manger, the baby curled in beautiful detail at the center. The wood had been rubbed to a sheen in the years that Krampus had held and loved it, caressing it every night before sleep with fingers that knew each detail by heart. Jesus's tiny hand was in the air, reaching. His eyes were open, looking at Agios.

"He's dead, son," Agios said.

"Jesus live. He . . . heals. Heals me. I end here. I go with him."

His mind is wandering. God, if you are real—if you are there—this is the cruelest of all your lies!

"No," Agios said. "You're my friend—my son. You can't die now. You can't."

"Not afraid," Krampus said. "Remember, father." He said something that Agios couldn't catch.

"Tell me again!"

"Believe," Krampus said. And then he exhaled.

"No," Agios groaned. "No. Don't go."

What had lived in the contorted body was fast leaving it. Krampus's wrinkles smoothed and his features seemed lit by a gentle glow. There was a thin smile on his lips, and in his last words a note of—joy?

"Believe." Krampus's mouth formed the word, but there was no air in his lungs to give it voice.

Agios shook. How many years ago had he closed his real son's eyes? With trembling fingers, he gently shut Krampus's eyelids now. "My son," he sobbed. Then, choking, he groaned, "My son." He looked up at the dark sky and in a voice ragged with anguish cried, "Why?"

No voice from on high answered him. There came only a thin echo of his own despair:

Why?

Agios traveled with Krampus slung over the back of their mule. He had to tie his friend's body in place, looping straps around his arms so his fingers wouldn't graze the ground. It was a grisly task made even more difficult by grief. He felt like a shell, as brittle and empty as a husk that would soon disappear in the wind.

Believe.

Agios couldn't. Not anymore.

Near midnight of their second day out of Jerusalem, Agios found the place. The night was dark, but a half moon cast enough light that Agios could just make out the familiar surroundings. He left Krampus and the mule at the foot of a cliff and climbed up a track that led through a narrow ravine. His pulse pounded, making the spear-cut on his face ache.

He heard a sound like thunder ahead, and when he turned the last bend he saw the abrupt end of the trail. Moisture in the air drifted in, cool on the skin. Agios inched forward and looked out. To his left a waterfall roared over a notch in the mountain rim. It fell thirty feet or more into a deep raging cauldron of white water, dashing high into the air again when the current met jagged rocks thrusting up from the riverbed.

They had found this place on one of their trading expeditions, and Agios had never forgotten the feeling it evoked.

He kicked a loose stone, and it tumbled down, vanishing

in the mist and spray before striking the bottom. If he took one step—

Certain death.

He had a promise to keep.

It didn't take long for Agios to undo the leather straps that lashed Krampus to the mule. He gently lowered the body to the ground, then knotted the straps together to create a rope long enough for his purposes. He looped the leather and threw it over his shoulder. Kneeling down to take the pouch from Krampus's neck, he removed the little carved baby and put it in his friend's big hand. He closed the fingers over it and bound them tight with the thong.

With a grunt, Agios lifted Krampus, throwing him over his shoulder like a lamb. His friend wasn't nearly as heavy as he had once been, but the burden weighed down on Agios as he stumbled up the ravine to the cliff edge.

In the notch of the ravine, with the great waterfall thundering off to his left, Agios set the body down and tied the leather rope securely around Krampus's torso, leaving several feet free. He weighted the big body with stones laced inside Krampus's clothing. Then Agios doubled his legs and tied the trailing rope around his own ankles so tightly that they bit his skin. Agios leaned over Krampus and said hoarsely, "My son, I will bury you in water, as you asked. I won't say farewell. I take this final journey with you."

He braced his back against the rocky wall of the ravine, put his feet against Krampus's back, and shoved as hard as he could. Krampus tumbled out into the air, and not a heartbeat later the rope jerked Agios out of the notch, too. He felt himself plunging, saw a blur of water and stone. He did not cry out.

Like a man, he did not cry out. Like Philos.

Agios of the frankincense, father to Philos, friend of Krampus, protector, carver, wanderer, follower of Jesus, fell. But his last thought was not of any of these things. It was of the Sychar well.

Living water.

PART II

Chapter 15

Snow assaulted Agios in the high pass, not the soft drifting flakes of the river valleys, but shattered windblown fragments of ice edged like knives. His eight dogs hunched their shoulders as they leaned into the blast and heaved the sledge over the rise of the ridge. Agios felt the balance shift, then they slanted downhill and toward the dark line of upland pines.

For a moment he glimpsed a break in the clouds off to the west, but other than that faint streak of light, the sky stretched heavy and gray. Above the tree line the mountain slopes lay locked in cold, the snow beneath the runners crusted into a steep sheet of ice. Instead of laboring to pull the sledge, the dogs ran with a grim determination to out-speed it, not to be overtaken and crushed. Within his layers of furs Agios hardly felt the savage mountain air, except for his exposed eyes, nose, and cheeks.

He had expected it. Agios had known how grueling the route would be, but his quarry roamed in small herds, alert to any human's approach, and this approach from above and downwind was the only way. The sledge picked up speed. Falling snow had coated its sturdy structure of prime cedar overlaid with pelts lashed down by cords of sinew. Agios knew just how much the sledge could take without tipping or breaking a runner. He had built it himself.

He had become ever more skilled with his hands in the decades that had passed since the waterfall, since throwing himself toward the death that eluded him. He had much time to practice—by his uncertain count 200 years and more, perhaps 250.

Agios never knew how long he spent under the waterfall tied to Krampus's body, but a time came when light dispersed the churning darkness. He had survived the night. Underwater, he had survived. His carving knife was still in his belt and he used it to saw through the leather cord that bound his legs. And then Agios was floating up, drawn heavenward though he felt marked for hell. What strange power was this?

It is a miracle. I wanted to beg one for Krampus—but it came to me instead.

To Agios, who did not want to accept the gift of life.

And his mission? God had rejected him. He would reject God and all mankind.

The mule had waited for him. He plodded away with it, aimless again, heading ever northward, for weeks, months, and then years. He did not want this life, and over the decades, whenever grief overcame him he sought death in other ways—by freezing cold and burning fire—but though he felt great pain, and always lost consciousness, he always awakened as if the miracle had happened all over again.

But for all his will to die, Agios learned that men's souls were bred for survival. He still, impossibly, found moments of wonder. Awe took him the first time he saw lights shimmering in the northern sky like flowers spilled from the heavens. The feeling of his own body straining to run, to fly, his muscles burning as he pushed himself to do *more*, could astonish him. Agios didn't know why he still drew breath, but sometimes the why of it didn't matter. He lived and could do nothing about that—except live as best he could.

Somehow vigor had returned to him, and he no longer felt the weight of age. Another part of the miracle, he supposed. He did feel the cold, though. The sledge hissed along. Wind-lashed snow stung his cheeks and nose. He could do nothing about that, so he ignored it.

He entered a sheltering region of pine and stunted hemlock, and the snow cover beneath the runners became looser, like sand instead of frozen water. Agios knew he would find his quarry farther downslope, beneath the mountain oaks. Still, he let the team slow, something the dogs had earned after the painful haul up to the pass and their hurried run down.

They breathed hard, pale white streamers puffing from their snouts and panting mouths. Agios shifted the reins and then slipped one hand from its heavy glove and reached to knead his nose until he had driven out the first signs of frostbite. Sensation stabbed back with a rush of pain that made his eyes water. Before donning the glove again, Agios ran his fingers over the scar that led from the bridge of his nose down across his left cheek.

It always made him think of Golgotha and what had ended there.

At last the sledge edged out onto a relatively flat expanse—not the base of the mountain, but the broad crest of another ridge tilting gently westward and downward along its southern flank—and below Agios saw the skeletal fingers of bare branches clutched dark against the white.

There he would find his prey.

He halted the sledge in the sheltering lee of a boulder. The dogs dropped to their bellies, chests heaving as they panted. Agios reached into a leather pouch and produced strips of dried smoked meat, venison from a stag brought down weeks before. He distributed it among the dogs, and they devoured it quickly. He did not speak to them. They knew their jobs and had no need for words. For their part, the well-trained dogs did not growl or bark. Each dog received a fair share of the meat, and each ate it in silence. Agios made sure they had all finished and then took off their harness. They would not scatter or wander. They owed Agios loyalty and obedience and were all the best at what they did.

As Agios unharnessed the last dog, something stirred in the swaths of lashed pelts, and a puppy emerged from the coverings. She was the only survivor of a litter of six, and she stared up at Agios with wide, brown eyes. Agios smiled and gave her a piece of dried venison. To say that Agios loved his dogs would have been a stretch. Still, this puppy's indomitable spirit captivated him. He had fed her with a rag soaked in goat's milk after her mother died, and she still slept curled up beside him at night. She would be a fine sled dog. The best.

Then Agios busied himself unlashing a pack, a leather bundle as tall as a man and nearly as bulky. The day had begun to fail. The weather would soon change. Very far to the west the break in the clouds grew and spread. Now he could see a thin rim of pale blue sky, and in one spot the sinking sun brightened it to silver. Other than that, the slate-gray snow clouds hung nearly low enough to brush the mountain peaks. They hid everything else overhead. The widening break in the clouds hinted the snowfall would cease that night, and that the stars might appear.

Agios sat on an exposed boulder to strap on his snow-shoes, cedar frames he himself had carved and bent and strung with sinews. He heaved up the pack, taking its burden on his shoulders, and then reached for the deadly spear. His work lay downslope.

Agios sniffed the air. He had reached the winter feeding grounds of the wild swine. Boars and sows had broken the trails, and judging from unfrozen dung, some had passed not long before. He followed a boar track to the edge of a clearing, a place frequented by the wild herd. Their comings and goings had trampled the snow. He expected some of them to appear before long, since a day earlier he had spotted a group of three sows and fifteen piglets. They slept through much of the day and woke to forage in the afternoon and into the night. Boars usually roamed apart from the rest, but this herd included a two-year-old male of a good size and weight. For some reason it stayed close to its mother.

The boar was old enough to respond to a challenge, inexperienced enough to fall victim to a hunter's trick. Agios rapidly emptied the pack. It contained flexible, tough strips of willow that he had painstakingly carved and contoured. He strapped them together to make a frame, and then adjusted a boar's pelt over it. This, his invention, had allowed him to take many animals that other hunters would never have attempted, not if they hunted alone, and not if they valued their lives.

He slipped beneath the structure, drew his bronze knife,

and made sure his spear was within reach. By manipulating rods attached to the joints he could make the boar seem to root in the leaves, look around, raise or lower a foreleg.

From his hiding place, Agios craned his neck to stare downslope. The sun was close to setting, which meant that the wild pigs must have started their nightly search for food. Though the trees gave protection from the worst of the weather, a breeze still blew in his face, and he could smell the animals. Before long he could also hear them grunting and scuffling. As twilight came on, they wandered into the clearing, where sows and piglets began to nose under the snow, into the leaf mold, searching for acorns, dormant grubs, and roots.

The boar came with them. He already stayed a little apart from the others. In the spring he would mate and then leave for the solitary life of a mature boar.

If he lived.

Agios grunted and made a snort. The boar turned sharply, ears up, muscles tense.

Boars had poor eyesight, but in the forest gloom this one was close enough to glimpse what looked like a rival. Agios made his decoy shake its head, made it paw the earth. He imitated the squeal of an angry boar.

His prey bristled, raised its shoulders, and returned the challenge. Then it leaped forward, breasting the snow, spraying it right and left as the barrel chest broke the surface. At the last moment, Agios rolled to his left, planted the butt of the boar spear against a root he had already found with his foot, and raised the steel point to meet the charge.

The boar saw something was wrong, tried at the last second to leap clear, but the steel blade impaled him as he jumped, plunged through flesh and sinew, broke bone, and sank deep. The boar toppled sideways, kicking and squealing. The other wild swine stampeded down the track, vanishing in the murk of the trees.

Agios used his knife to slash the boar's throat. The animal twitched, gurgled, and died, its hot blood jetting and steaming in the icy air.

He dragged the dead weight of the carcass to a spot beneath a sturdy limb, threw a stout rope up and over the branch, hauled the boar up, dangling by its front legs, and with his bronze knife quickly and deftly opened the carcass. The guts spilled out, stinking, splattering the snow. With the efficiency of an expert butcher Agios dismembered the boar: meat enough for a month. He hung the cuts of pork out of the reach of predators. A boar this size would weigh twice what a man did. Agios planned to bring the sledge down to load the meat and pelt, though that might take some time.

Done with his butchering, he wiped spear and knife, took the decoy apart, repacked everything, and hefted the sack. He started back up the slope. He realized then how little time the whole act of slaughter and butchery had taken. The sun still rested on the very rim of the world, just below the far edge of the snow clouds, and a strip of red sky made everything the color of bronze.

Before Agios cleared the last oaks, he heard sounds that made his heart thud and yanked him from his reverie: yelps and frenzied snarls, barks of defiance and shrieks of wounded dogs. He had seen no sign of—*wolves!*

Agios dropped the pack, slashed the lashings of his snowshoes, and broke into an adrenaline-fueled run, making straight for the sledge, both spear and knife gripped in his bare hands. His heart pounded harder when, in the softer snow, he spotted a confusion of fresh tracks.

Yes. Wolves!

Cold burned his lungs as he clambered up the steepest part of the slope, the shortest route. He met one of his dogs, its left hind leg bloody and trailing. It whimpered.

Agios burst into the sheltered place where he had left the sledge. It had been dragged some distance and lay overturned, the pelts scattered. Four of his dogs lay ripped and bloody, dead on the snow.

The pup was gone.

Agios reeled, hands to his head as he absorbed this fresh loss. If there was one thing that he had learned in his weary pilgrimage, it was that death followed him wherever he went. It was why he hadn't spoken to a person in more years than he could count. He wasn't entirely sure his voice still worked or how to address another human being. He had become wholly and unconditionally alone in a world that had utterly forsaken him. His last connection to human feeling was his attachment to his animals.

Agios couldn't hold the cry that welled up in his throat, born of grief that stretched back over two hundred years, to a life he remembered like a bad dream. *Had* he dreamed it, the nightmare of loss and death?

When he screamed, he sounded exactly like a tormented wild animal. Injured, broken—but unable to die.

Surely, that was the worst fate of all.

Chapter 16

✦

Agios left the mountains. Four or six or more generations of men ago, he had banished himself from the world, trying to find peace, but now . . . With his three surviving dogs he journeyed over treacherous mountain passes. Agios felt unworthy of their loyalty, but they flanked him like guards, one on either side, the third bringing up the rear.

Agios had always named his dogs by some descriptive term—Gray Shadow, Trotter, Leaper, Sly, Fighter—and his surviving animals were Tracker, Gentle, and Brave Dog. Brave Dog was his rear guard and he trailed his fingers along Tracker's head as he walked.

For days they hiked the barren, rocky peaks, hiding under outcroppings in the jagged rock when storms raged overhead. Agios brought down small game for them in the evenings. He was grateful for the warmth of his dogs; their bodies beside him were a comfort. He knew that with or without them he would survive, but the thought gave him no satisfaction.

Agios had somehow been plucked from the human race, set apart for some purpose he could not understand. *Why me?* he had wondered a million times. *Why not Philos or Krampus or . . . Jesus?* At first, Agios had even tried to pray, but since he felt no response, he had gradually ceased. What god would do this to him? Curse him with life that would not end, life filled only with two imperatives, survival and regret. He would do so much differently if he had the chance, starting with drinking the water at the Sychar well—and taking Jesus's words to heart. He could still change, he thought, but no, impossible. He had become too set in his ways, and no god could forgive him for all the mistakes he had made over the years. No god could forgive a man who'd sent his own son to die in unimaginable pain on a tree.

He touched the scar on his cheek, the brand of his shame. *I wasn't worthy of my mission. I failed. And now I'm cursed.*

When Agios and his dogs left the snowy passes for a gentler clime, when the earth began to green again and the spindly shrubs of rocky soil became tall pines with long needles the color of spring grass and bay trees thick with their distinctive spearhead leaves, he still had no destination in mind. He was in a country near the sea, he knew that. Maybe eventually he would travel farther south, find himself among men again. Or maybe not. He began to look around for some place to live.

He found a cave eroded into the side of a squat mountain. Agios had lived in many caves in the weary decades and even centuries after the death of Jesus, and he made quick work of domesticating this one. Sand floor, low ceiling, drafty but safe. He gathered wood, swept pine needles into a bed, and dug a fire pit, lining it with flat stones. An oil lamp he hung on a spiked rock near the door, and his tools he laid carefully in the back corner. He had not lighted the lamp for many years—for no olives grew in the farthest north—but he had seen wild olive trees in this southern countryside, and the light would be welcome.

The dogs ranged around the mountainside, full of life and excited by the green surroundings. They were used to a harsher world, and to be in a place where warmth replaced cold, and life took the place of barrenness, seemed to please them. Yes, this would do for a while, anyway.

That night Agios lit a small fire in the pit outside his cave and with his dogs at his side studied the stars. He scanned the skies for something different, but no new star had appeared in nearly three hundred years. No angelic light shone for him. The world had changed. The stars and Agios had not. But as Agios watched, a single point of light shimmered bright and broke loose from the canvas of the night, streaking across the darkness like a banner. What did it proclaim?

Maybe something was about to change after all.

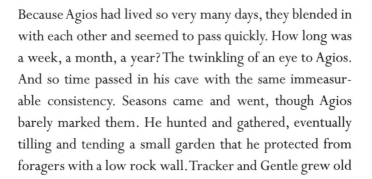

Because Agios had lived so very many days, they blended in with each other and seemed to pass quickly. How long was a week, a month, a year? The twinkling of an eye to Agios. And so time passed in his cave with the same immeasurable consistency. Seasons came and went, though Agios barely marked them. He hunted and gathered, eventually tilling and tending a small garden that he protected from foragers with a low rock wall. Tracker and Gentle grew old and died, and Agios buried them beyond the garden and marked their graves with stones. Brave Dog was the only companion that Agios had left in the world. Still, he didn't leave the mountain to seek out other people.

Then one spring, the verdant valley below his home became grazing fields for a small herd of sheep. The first morning that Agios awoke to find the landscape dotted with their white, woolly forms, his heart leaped into his throat. *Go*, he thought, for when he thought he was near men, his immediate impulse always turned to flight.

But in the distance he saw a shepherd—only a little boy—who waved to him from perhaps two thousand yards away. Almost against his will, Agios raised his hand in greeting, too. There was no danger, so long as the shepherd stayed away.

All that spring the little shepherd tended his sheep, letting them graze on the lower shoulders of the mountain during the day and collecting them safely together at night. His camp was out of sight, but every morning he returned to the valley. He had two dogs, similar in size and appearance to Brave Dog, and Agios could tell that his own companion longed to go make friends. But Brave Dog was too well trained. He wouldn't leave Agios's side.

And one morning as summer blazed hot the shepherd did not come, nor did his flocks.

Agios didn't mean to grieve. What had he lost? They had never even exchanged a word. But all the same, the night after his young neighbor had gone away, Agios sat alone at his fire with a knife in his hand. He carved a perfect sheep. A pair of them, actually: a pretty little ewe with wide, doe eyes and a ram with proudly curved horns. Agios's hands had gained cunning over the long years, and these were beautiful creatures. He set them gently on a stone shelf in his cave.

The shepherd came back with the turn of the next winter to early spring. It was around noon on a beautiful, sun-bright day when the first sheep wandered into view. Agios was weeding his garden, and when he stood to stretch his back and caught sight of the familiar puff of white against the new green grass, he felt his heart swell. *Ridiculous*, he chastised himself. *Foolish to be so smitten with a lamb.* However, the shepherd, not his sheep, was what made his heart beat faster. Agios was reluctant to admit it, but he longed for human contact.

That night, when the shepherd and his flock were sleeping, Agios crept down the slope. In each hand he carried a humble offering. Just as in the old days, he didn't wish to give his gift outright. Instead, he found a wide, flat rock under a tree where he had often seen the boy rest in the midday heat. There he placed the ram and his ewe, head to head as if nuzzling each other. A smile shadowed his face as he returned to his cave.

Then three days later Agios brought a burden home, a load of wood—some of it fuel for his fire, some carefully selected material for his carving. He dumped the wood into a lidless bin he had shaped from dry-laid stone. He lit the oil lamp—he cultivated and pressed olives now, more for their oil than for their value as food—and the yellow glow brightened the recesses of the cave. Then he sorted out the carving wood into a separate stack, and at last straightened and dusted his hands.

And then he heard it: a clattery little sound, the sound of wood clicking on wood.

It came from within the side cavern where he stored his carvings. In the year since he had carved the ewe and ram, he had revived his old pastime. He had stored scores of carvings there, all done since he had first carved the sheep. Quietly, his footfalls silent on the sandy floor, Agios crossed, ducked low at the arched entrance, and looked in.

A black-haired boy in shepherd's clothes—a plain knee-length tunic of brown wool and sandals—sat cross-legged on the sandy ground, pushing a carved wagon along the floor. The wheels turned, and the oxen's legs moved. Brave Dog lay on his stomach nearby, his tail thumping. The boy was so engrossed in the toy that he didn't even glance around.

It was his shepherd, the boy on the hill who had waved the first day they spotted each other over a year earlier. Agios felt his chest fill with conflicting emotions: dread that the child had reached out, elation that he was here. Fear and surprise. Joy.

Agios cleared his throat. "Who are you?" he asked in Aramaic. His own voice was rough and unfamiliar in his ears.

In the dim light that filtered in from the main cave, the boy looked around over his shoulder, his brown eyes wide with surprise. He had a shy smile. In Koine Greek, he said, "Hello. I'm Nicholas. Who are you?"

Agios nodded at the wagon and answered in the boy's language: "I'm the man who made that."

"It's beautiful," Nicholas said, reaching over to scratch Brave Dog's ears. "Did you make the ewe, too? And the ram?" He stood up and produced the carvings from his pockets.

Agios nodded, noticing the top of the boy's head was bald.

Very seriously, the boy asked, "Sir, have you seen a lamb? He's about three months old, and I've lost him. He's white. I mean, well, of course he's white. After all, he's a lamb."

Agios shook his head, though his mouth wanted to twitch into a smile at the boy's grave words and attitude. How old was the lad? Eight? Nine? Very young indeed. "I've seen no lamb. What happened to your hair?"

Nicholas smiled and touched the spot with his fingers. "It's a tonsure. My uncle—his name is Nicholas, too—is a priest and he hopes I'll be one. He did this when I came to stay with him and learn from him. All priests have their heads shaved like this."

"Aren't you a little young to be a priest?" Agios asked curtly.

The boy tried to stand taller. "I'm almost eleven!"

Agios asked, "Where's your uncle?"

Nicholas pointed, though he probably had no real sense of direction here in the inner cave. "He's about two miles away, with the other shepherds. Down lower. There's more grazing in the foothills."

Agios frowned. "He's a shepherd? I thought you said he was a priest."

"And a shepherd, too," the boy said. He sighed. "It's my fault, losing the lamb. I felt drowsy and closed my eyes and when I woke up, all the sheep were there but that one. I shouldn't have let the lamb get away. Now I've got to find it and bring it home."

"So much trouble over one lamb," Agios said.

"But it's *my* lamb. It's my responsibility," the boy replied.

Agios stooped to pick up the wagon and its oxen. "Then I suppose we'd better go look for it."

The boy sounded discouraged. "I can't find any sign of him, and I've already looked all the way up to this meadow. He's been gone since dawn, and it's after noon now."

"What makes you think he'd be here?"

"He's a climber," Nicholas said. "He likes to be in high places. My uncle says he's part mountain goat. I think he'd go uphill, that's all."

Agios thought that the boy should know his own sheep well enough to be right about that. He said, "We'll start here, then, and look a little harder. Are you hungry?"

"No," the boy said, but his voice was hesitant.

"You can't go hunting on an empty stomach."

"I have nothing to pay you with."

Agios shook his head at that and gave him some food anyway, a small bowl full of a cold stew of goat's meat, lentils, and onions, and Nicholas wolfed it down as Brave Dog ate his own meal. When he finished, Agios said, "Let's go. Stay, Brave Dog."

"Can't he go with us?"

"He's old and tired and it's better for him to guard the cave," Agios said, not mentioning the fact that the dog had accepted Nicholas without trying to frighten him off.

They looked through three of the small, high meadows and saw only a few wild goats, a hare or two, and the soaring eagles that nested in the mountains. Nicholas clearly felt discouraged, but Agios said, "Oh, don't lose hope, young fellow. The lamb's had a lot of time to climb, and we have to go slower. We'll find him, I think."

In fact Agios, the old hunter, had spotted some signs of the lamb that the boy missed: a little pile of dark greenish droppings, and then later some strands of white wool caught on a briar. Finally he imitated the bleat of a ewe, and they heard a faint, weak voice replying from some way off. "That will be your lamb," he told Nicholas.

"Why doesn't he come to us?"

"Maybe he can't. This way."

They talked as they searched, and Agios learned a little about the boy: He lived in Patara. His father was Epiphanius and his mother Johanna. Nicholas seemed surprised when Agios gave no sign of recognition. "My parents are well known in town."

"Why aren't you with them, then?" Agios asked. The boy squared his narrow shoulders. "In the spring I live with my uncle. He's my father's older brother. He's training me to be a priest. He taught me how to read and write, and I'm studying the scrolls my family owns. It's really my uncle's lamb I'm looking for, but he said if I'd raise it I could have it."

That brought Agios back to the task. He pointed uphill. "From the way he bleats and doesn't come, I suspect he's caught in a thicket I know about."

The ravine would be a torrent in times of flood, but on a dry day it was a crooked gully floored with loose pebbles and tough grass. At the upper end stood a stubborn growth of camelthorn, a snarl more than chest-high to Agios. From inside the thicket came the lamb's weak, hoarse bleats. The animal had tangled its wool in so many briars that it couldn't tear loose.

Agios drew his knife from its scabbard and cut the vines, working them free from the lamb's pelt. "Let him eat and drink and I'll see you back to your people."

"You've scratched up your hands," Nicholas said.

The backs of Agios's hands were crisscrossed with bloody streaks, but they didn't hurt. The scars he had earned over the long years had been some protection. "They'll heal," Agios told Nicholas. "Let's see if this little fellow can walk."

The lamb seemed exhausted, staggering and falling to its knees, so Agios picked it up and shouldered it, the animal's hind legs on his left side and the forelegs on the right, its belly warm against the back of his neck. They reached a trickling stream of good water, and the lamb drank and seemed a little better. Lower still, it grazed for a while on tender new grass, and then Agios picked him up again.

The sun had slipped halfway down the sky by the time they reached the lower meadows. Nicholas was nimble-footed, and they went far down the slopes until Agios saw the blue drift of smoke from a campfire in a green clearing a mile or so away. He set the lamb down, and after its rest on his shoulders, it began to frisk around.

"Watch him closer in the future," Agios advised.

"Come into our camp," Nicholas said. "I'm sure my uncle will want to reward you. He'll feed you, at least."

The boy's kindness stabbed Agios, hurting him more than the sharp thorns had. "No, I don't have good luck among people," Agios said with a secretly bitter smile. *Or among priests*, he added mentally.

"Could I come and visit you again?"

"That wouldn't be wise," Agios said, trying to sound discouraging. "I'm a hermit, you see, living all by myself. I don't like company." When the boy looked disappointed, he relented a little: "Well, I won't forbid you, but don't come often. Visiting me can be very dangerous—for reasons you can't know. Take your lamb and get back to your flocks and your uncle now."

He turned and walked away with a quick pace and did not pause or look back for a long way. When he scaled a high ridge and stared back down the mountain, he could barely make out the thin wisp of smoke from the shepherds' campfire, and he saw no sign of Nicholas or his lamb.

Chapter 17

A gios hoped—though he wouldn't have admitted it—
that he would see Nicholas again. That night he began
carving another gift for this boy who was the closest thing to
a friend that he had encountered in too many weary years.
Something inside Agios had awakened in the presence of
the child. Maybe it was his memory of Philos, or Krampus,
or even Jesus. No matter. Agios bitterly reminded himself
that those he let himself care for always died.

Still, he set to work carving a trio of camels, one bending to drink at an invisible oasis, a second arching its neck
proudly, and the third with legs splayed in a wild, desert
run. *Why these?* he wondered, and the answer came from

somewhere: *Because Nicholas seems to be a seeker, like Caspar, Balthasar, and Melchior. But like them and all men, he is doomed to disappointment.*

Two months later, near the end of the grazing season, Agios walked by moonlight to the same place where he had left the carved ewe and set down the camels. Let the boy find them and play. Growing up would gradually rob him of the wonder and joy that Agios had heard in his voice. Let him at least have pleasant times to remember.

The shepherds and their flocks returned the following spring, and Agios felt his heart lift at the sight of sheep once again in the valley. It was the third year that they had graced his mountain, and if Agios remembered correctly, Nicholas would be twelve years old—or almost.

Agios didn't approach them, but he couldn't help hoping against his will—and his warning—that maybe his path would cross Nicholas's again.

A morning came when Agios sat outside the cave, in the shade of a dwarfish fig tree, carving a fisherman who would, when finished, hold and cast a small net woven of woolen strands. He was working on the figure's face, which demanded concentration and a steady hand. In the same moment he became aware of someone watching him, he also realized that the boy, standing quiet on the edge of his vision, had probably been there for a long time.

He glanced up, his white beard barely concealing a smile. "Hello, Nicholas."

"Hello," the boy said. He stood to one side, silent as a stone, and he carried a bundle tied with crisscrossing twine. He held it out. "This is for you. Because you helped me that time when the lamb ran off."

"Oh, that was nothing. I didn't want any reward for that," Agios said, but now he couldn't stop himself from smiling at the boy's earnest face and serious voice.

Nicholas looked a little downcast at Agios's refusal. He held the bundle out farther and said more softly, "Please, take it. I meant it for you."

"Well, well, let's see what it is." Agios carefully set aside his knife and the figure he was carving and took the bundle. Someone had done an expert job of binding it with the tied twine, and he quickly undid the knot. He shook it out and found it was a knee-length jacket, woven of wool and dyed red, trimmed with white. Agios smiled and shook his head.

"Nicholas, I just took a short walk up the mountain with you. This is too much to repay such a small favor."

"No," Nicholas insisted. "It was my grandfather's, but it was too big for my father to wear and it's just been folded in a chest for years. My mother said I could give it away to someone who needed it. I thought you—might get cold in the winter sometimes."

Agios stood and tried on the garment. It was a perfect fit. He took it off again and held it out, admiring it. "Well. Sometimes the winter winds are sharp here. It's a very good coat. Thank you, and thank your mother for me. I can't go hunting in this, though. The quarry would spot me from miles off, this red color against the brown of the mountains." When Nicholas looked disappointed, Agios added, "I'll always wear it when I'm not hunting, though, and the north wind is blowing cold. It'll be welcome then. How is your lamb?"

"He's a yearling now," Nicholas said, looking happier. He sat on a stone near Agios, his face lit up with enthusiasm. Brave Dog, feeling his years, came halting out of the cave—he must have scented or heard Nicholas—and settled at the boy's feet. Nicholas leaned to pat him as he continued: "He's a lot bigger than he was. His horns are coming in nicely and he's already butting heads with other little rams. What are you making now?"

Agios picked up the little figurine he'd been working on. "This will be a fisherman. When I finish, he'll be able to hold on to a fishing net. You can flick a lever in his back and he'll toss the net out. I mean to carve three little fish that he can catch, too."

"I will make you fishers of men," Nicholas said absently, studying Agios's fine handiwork.

Agios felt as if he had been struck. Something about those words was a blow to his soul. "What did you say?" he asked, but his breath was gone in his chest and he barely wheezed the words.

Nicholas looked up and wrinkled his nose impishly. "Just something my uncle read to me," he said. Then, oblivious to Agios's discomfort, he prattled on, "I've seen fishermen. Every day they go out in boats from the port. I've never fished, though. Have you?"

"Not in the ocean," Agios managed. He forced himself to focus on the carving in his hands. He sighed and added, "I'm pretty good at spearing them in the mountain pools, though."

"I've never done that, either," Nicholas told him. "Some of the other shepherds do, but not me."

"Anyone could teach you."

The boy thought about this. "I don't think so," he said at last. "I don't think I'd like killing things, even if they're just fish. I don't help out when the sheep have to be slaughtered because I don't like it. But I eat fish and mutton. Is that wrong?"

"I wouldn't say so," Agios told him. "Their purpose in life is to be food."

They were silent for a few moments while Agios picked up his tools again and resumed careful work on the fisherman. He let Nicholas crane his neck and watch, and tilted his hands so that the boy could see the fine detail, the razor-sharp tip of the tiny pick he used to create wrinkles and features in a face as small as his thumb.

"You're really good at that," Nicholas said after a while.

Agios didn't respond. True, he was very skilled. But he had had a very long time to practice. After a while he asked, carefully, "Do you like learning from your uncle?"

He felt rather than saw Nicholas nod. "He's a good man. I'm named after him, you know."

Agios didn't know, but he didn't point that out.

"Uncle Nicholas says that God has a plan for me."

Agios caught Nicholas's eye and smiled. It didn't matter what he personally believed or didn't believe about God. This child was a wonder. "I'm sure he does. A magnificent plan." *He just doesn't have one for me.* The thought came unbidden and Agios had to fight the wave of sadness that washed over him.

"I'm going to be a bishop one day and tell people the Good News." The boy whispered the words as if they were a secret, but he sat up a little straighter, his eyes shining.

Agios had heard enough to know that the God Nicholas spoke of was the Hebrew God, and he wanted to hear no more about the one who had filled him with such hope— and then allowed Jesus to die so cruelly on a cross.

Nicholas said he had to go. Agios walked partway down the mountain with him, and when they reached a stand of black pines, he paused and said, "Again, I thank you for the gift, young Nicholas. But it would be better if you didn't come back. Bad things happen to the people I . . ." Agios faltered and then began again. "Bad things always happen to the people I care about."

"I'm not afraid," Nicholas assured him with a broad smile, and then he went on his way, pausing once to wave farewell.

Months after that, in the high blaze of a summer day, Brave Dog barked, drawing Agios's attention to someone who was climbing the mountainside. The man did not seem used to the mountains. He toiled his way up the steep track, leaning on a stick of wood he had picked up somewhere, and as he came closer, he held out a scrap of parchment. "Nicholas, the son of Epiphanius, sent me to you with this," he said. "I left yesterday morning and got here hours ago, but I couldn't find your cave."

"Who are you?" Agios repeated, taking the parchment from him.

"I was a helper of the shepherd Nicholas the Priest," the stranger told him, crossing himself.

"Was?"

The man looked ready to weep. "He's dead. I have to go." He started away, then turned for a moment to look back. "There's a plague in the town," he said. "I don't dare return there. I'll camp in the fields where the sheep graze in spring."

Agios looked at the words written on the parchment. The message was short but urgent: *Please come.*

No name, but the words were in an unformed, childish handwriting: Nicholas.

Agios hurried back to the cave, took a few of his belongings in a sack, and then went out and opened the pen so the goats would be able to find pasturage. He left food and water for Brave Dog. It was after sunset when he set off on the long journey to Patara. All night he walked, and for some reason this time he felt his years. Perhaps, he thought, the dread of what he might find in the town pressed on him.

A lone guard stood at the town gate as Agios approached in the coolness of dawn. When the man challenged him, Agios said, "I mean no harm. There is sickness in the town. I have come to offer what help I can."

The guard hesitated, but then waved him in and told him where to find the house of Epiphanius.

It was earliest morning, but few stirred in Patara. As he walked through the streets, Agios heard again and again the muffled sounds of wailing. He saw people kneeling on the steps of a church and heard the murmur of their prayers.

Agios found the home of Epiphanius and knocked on the door, but no one appeared to let him in. He tried the door and found it unlocked. Young Nicholas, his face tight with strain, his eyes dark with lack of sleep, met him in the hallway and said, "My mother and father are very sick."

He led Agios to their bedroom. They lay together in one bed, neither of them fully conscious, both burning with fever. Agios said, "I'll do what I can." He led Nicholas to the front door and took the boy by the shoulders. "Listen to me," he said, looking into the tired eyes. "I want you to go to my cave and stay there. You'll find plenty of food. The goats will need milking and tending, and Brave Dog will need to be fed. Do this for me, and if I can, I'll help your parents."

"So many people are sick," Nicholas said miserably. "My uncle—" He gulped and pointed at a closed door. "He's in there. He's dead."

"Say prayers for him and your parents," Agios said urgently. "But go now. Do as I say and you'll be safe. I'll bring you word as soon as I can. Hurry!"

Nicholas looked frightened, but he nodded and ran.

None of the servants had stayed in the house of sickness, not one. Agios managed everything himself, and when he heard a bell ringing outside, he went into the street and found a funeral procession, a priest leading a small party of mourners and a shrouded body lying on a cart. "Is one of you a priest?" he asked.

The funeral party stopped, and one of the men stepped forward. "Yes. I am," he said.

"Then when you have buried the dead, return here. We need you."

Before the priest returned, and before the hour passed, Johanna died. Agios lifted her—he did not fear the disease himself, for what could it do to a man who could not die?—and carried her body to the room where the corpse of Nicholas the priest lay.

Not long after that, the priest who had led the funeral procession knocked at the door. Agios let him in. "I'm Agios, a friend of this family," he told the priest.

"I'm Father Eudemus," the man said—a young man, with a tonsure shaved in his hair, like Nicholas and his uncle.

"Father?" Agios asked, surprised.

The priest nodded. "Do you not know Christian customs? 'Father' is a title we give to priests. How is the family?"

"Nicholas the priest and Johanna are dead," Agios told him. "Epiphanius has a bad fever and seems in pain."

They sponged the suffering man while Father Eudemus explained the course of the illness: It had come, he said, over the sea, aboard a ship from Tyre. The disease had broken out among those who worked in or lived near the harbor. From there it had spread like a wildfire.

Father Eudemus lamented the death of Nicholas the priest. "He was a good man and a brave one. When few of us dared to go among the ill to offer help and prayer, he was the first. Surely Jesus will welcome him home."

Agios started at the name, but clamped his lips tightly. This was no time for questions. Epiphanius weakened through the day. In his fever he babbled and murmured bits of prayers, calling on Jesus. The priest asked Agios to step outside while he heard the dying man's last confession.

Nicholas's father lasted only about another hour after that. Almost at sunset he opened his eyes and saw Agios. "The man with the white beard. My son spoke of you," he croaked. Though he was still in the grip of a burning fever, he shivered and murmured something too softly for Agios to hear. "Listen—take the Gospel scrolls for him. Father Eudemus will show you where they are." He murmured something too low for Agios to hear.

"Say it again," Agios told him gently, bending to bring his ear close to the dying man's lips.

"Be a father to my son," Epiphanius whispered, and then he was gone. The priest made the sign of the cross over his body—as he had done for Johanna and Nicholas the elder—and said, "Now they are with God."

Agios remained in town even after their funerals, helping as much as he could. The plague raged for ten further days. On the third, Father Eudemus himself fell ill, and Agios took the care of his sick parishioners on himself. Many died, but others lived. Father Eudemus was one of the fortunate ones.

The new infections began to trail off on the fifth day, and by the ninth only those who had caught the illness earlier lingered. The next morning Agios told Father Eudemus, who was still not strong enough to get out of bed, that he was going to see about young Nicholas. He packed a bag with the scrolls that the priest showed him—they reminded him of the scholar-king Caspar—and then set out.

He found Nicholas weeping. Brave Dog had stopped eating. He thumped his tail once when Agios knelt by him. "He is very old," Agios said. "He knows it's his time to— go and join his brothers. Nicholas, I have something to tell you."

Nicholas wept again at the news. Agios embraced him. At last the boy fell into a fitful sleep. When he woke, it was just in time to come and sit beside Agios as Brave Dog slipped away. "He was a good animal," Agios said, a silent tear running down his cheek. He gave the sack to Nicholas. "Here. Your father gives these to you."

"The Gospels," Nicholas said quietly. He swallowed and said, "I'll see my father and mother and uncle again one day. They're with Jesus now."

"Jesus is dead," he said softly. He placed both hands on Nicholas's shoulders, rooting him to the ground. "He died on a cross." Agios didn't say *I saw it happen*, for who could believe such folly? Nicholas would think he was insane.

"No," Nicholas said, and the hint of a smile touched his lips. "He's not dead at all. On the third day he rose, Agios. He *rose*."

Agios's breath stuck in his chest. The words were so un- complicated, so sweet and life-giving. *He rose*.

Wasn't it what he had longed for to ease all his terrible grief? For his beautiful wife, who had died far too early, to rise again, and their poor stillborn second son? For Philos, taken dead and bleeding from the libanos tree, to live again? For Krampus, gentle friend, his second son, to overcome death? The thought that Jesus had done what surely only he could do, that he had defeated even death and turned the world upside down, was a hope that floated from deep inside Agios and lifted his head to the heavens.

Nicholas looked up at him, smiling through his tears. "They will live forever now. The Gospels promise that."

Jesus had said it! *"The water I give them will become in them a spring of water welling up to eternal life."*

"I want to bury Brave Dog," he said, choking on his own rising hope. "Then—then I want you to explain these Gospels to me."

When they had covered Brave Dog's grave—Agios dug it between those of Tracker and the dog he had named Gentle for her sweet disposition—Nicholas took hold of his hand, offering comfort.

In the following days Agios felt poised between new hope and old despair. Nicholas read passages to him from the scrolls, and the boy obviously believed what they said. Was it true? Had Jesus truly risen again from the tomb? Was he waiting in heaven to reward those who believed in him and his Father?

"I go and prepare a place for you. And if I go, I will come again, and receive you unto myself; that where I am, there ye may be also."

Agios wept as he remembered Jesus's assurance to the thief crucified beside him: "Truly I tell you, today you will be with me in paradise."

Nicholas helped in every way he could, tending the flocks, even cooking. Then one day he came shyly to Agios and said, "This time I've made a gift for you." He offered it to Agios, and when the old man didn't reach for it, Nicholas took his friend by the hand and placed the object in his palm.

Agios examined the crude carving, turning it over and over in his fingers. The world had gone eerily quiet; the songs of the morning birds were silenced in his ears. He felt numb, as though swaddled in blankets so thick he could hardly feel the edges of the small block of wood in his hands. His mind simply couldn't comprehend what he was seeing.

The carving wasn't as good as his own, obviously a beginner's attempt, but there was no mistaking what it was. A baby. In a manger.

It was Jesus.

"Believe in him," Nicholas said gently.

It welled up within Agios then, all the longing, all the loss. Weala and the stillborn child, Philos, Jesus . . . and yes, Krampus, whispering with his dying breath that same word:

Believe.

Agios couldn't reply.

Chapter 18

✦

Agios had questions that Nicholas could not answer, so Agios consented to accompany his young friend to his father's home in Patara. He didn't want to leave this place of refuge, this place where he had opened himself up to friendship again, but one of Nicholas's answers had cut him to the core.

"Why did you not tell me earlier you followed Jesus?"

Nicholas looked genuinely confused. "We are a persecuted people, Agios. I've been dropping hints—fishers of men? Talk of the creator? Plans for hope and a future?—but I never dared to say anything outright. But you did a Christian thing in caring for my parents."

"Christian?"

"That means a follower of Christ," Nicholas said.

When Agios didn't seem to understand, Nicholas unlaced a pouch slung from his belt. All of the carvings that Agios had given him were inside it, and Nicholas went to his knees so that he could arrange them properly on the sandy ground just outside the cave. Three camels on the periphery, then the ram and ewe with heads bowed together. A cow and her calf side by side. In pride of place, a man and woman with their hands interlaced, a shepherd, and finally, in the center, the baby in a manger that Nicholas had carved himself.

It was the entire story, spread out before Agios. It was beautiful.

Then he frowned a little. He recalled the story the shepherd had told to the three scholar-kings, and how he had described the scene. "This is how it was," he said softly, reaching to move the cow and the calf to the other side and to place the sheep a little closer to Joseph. "There. Now I know why you carved Jesus in the manger."

Nicholas ducked his head. "I'm not very good."

"You'll be a fine carver, and a fine man," Agios said, and he meant it. "But what did you mean about followers of Jesus being persecuted?"

"You can learn that from the others in town."

And so it was settled. The two of them started out at once, walking all through the day, taking a meal while still on their feet and moving, never resting more than a few minutes at a time. The boy grew dazed with effort, but Agios steadied him and walked so that his shadow offered Nicholas some shade from the increasingly hot glare of the sun.

They headed down the slopes, at first through the stony passes through the mountains, then through grassy upland meadows, and at last through stands of black pines in the lower hills. The steep and winding track should have exhausted them, but Agios never felt the least weariness, and though Nicholas occasionally stumbled, he said nothing. He was young and had the endurance of youth—and its stubbornness as well, its reluctance to admit weakness. All that morning they walked, and then through a long, sweltering afternoon, and then past the setting of the sun.

They came at last to Patara in the darkness of late twilight. The two Roman guards at the gate recognized Nicholas, son of Epiphanius, and let them pass. A few people still were on the streets of the town, most of them hurrying to their homes, and Agios could smell the salty tang of the ocean on the evening air. Nicholas muttered, "This way," and led Agios through the twists and turns of the streets.

Only when they arrived at Nicholas's old home did Agios realize with a shock that he had completely worn the boy out with the long trip.

Nicholas could hardly stand upright, and his shoulders drooped as though he had been carrying a heavy weight the whole way. He unlocked the door and then showed Agios where his bedroom was, and Agios spread sheets on the bed for him. The house had a musty, closed-up scent, and Nicholas told Agios to light a candle.

It had been scented with tiny grains of . . . frankincense.

Someone knocked at the door a little after that. Agios opened it and found Father Eudemus and a woman. "I had word that you had brought Nicholas home," the priest said. "This woman, Nona, was a servant in the house. She will cook and clean for you, if you and the boy mean to stay."

"I have no money to pay her," Agios said.

The priest smiled. "Nicholas's father was very wealthy. I have his money. It goes to Nicholas now. I will pay her, if you wish. Would you like for Nona to prepare a meal for you and the boy?"

"He's asleep now, but in the morning—priest Eudemus, I must ask you. Nicholas told me something that surprised me. He spoke of Jesus of Nazareth—"

He broke off as Nona made an unusual gesture, touching her forehead, the center of her chest, left shoulder, and right shoulder.

"Go on," Eudemus said kindly.

"Come in, please. Nona, do you have a room?"

"Yes."

"Stay there for the night. I want to talk to this man."

She left them, and Agios led the priest to a room with shelves of scrolls. The two sat in chairs at the table, the priest at the head, Agios on his right. Agios said without preamble, "Nicholas tells me you follow the teachings of Jesus of Nazareth."

With a slight nod, the priest replied, "Yes, that's right. Although some would consider that a dangerous statement."

"Nicholas thinks it is. He says Christians are persecuted."

The priest's brows drew together in a frown. "We are falling out of favor with Diocletian. I fear the worst. We are blamed for anything and everything that goes wrong in Rome."

"Do you Christians actually plot against Rome?" Agios asked.

"Should I answer that?" Eudemus said, and this time his tone was serious and he did not smile.

Agios looked him in the eye. "Though I may be a stranger to you, I'm not a Roman spy. I told you I don't know anything. I ask for myself alone, not for others, and not from some evil motive."

Slowly Eudemus replied, "I meant no offense, Agios. You ask if we're really rebellious against the emperor. We've had reasons enough to rebel against the government, God knows. But no, we don't plan uprisings or revolts. You see, we're taught not to return violence for violence."

"Or evil for evil," Agios murmured, remembering the lesson poor Krampus had tried to teach him beside the Nile. "But Nicholas says the Romans enslave you and kill you!"

The priest replied, "This will be so hard for you to understand. Yes, the Romans think that they can kill us. In our opinion, that's impossible. If we believe in the promise of Christ, we won't die, but will have everlasting life."

"That's what I can't understand. Everyone dies," Agios said, suppressing the bitter thought: *Everyone except me.*

"When I say we won't die, I'm speaking of life beyond this world," Eudemus explained. "Our bodies perish, but our souls live on forever in the presence of God. It's why Jesus had to die on the cross, to offer us cleansing of sin and a way to God's glory. He conquered death, Agios. He holds the keys of death and hell."

That was more than Agios could take in. He thought quietly for a moment, then asked, "How did you learn of Jesus? I know that's a simple question, but I'm a simple man and need to start at the very beginning. Explain as you would for a child."

Eudemus raised his eyebrows. "Agios, that's really a profound way to begin, not simple at all. Jesus once told those who asked him about the secrets of heaven that they should become like little children."

Agios blinked back tears, thinking of Krampus, and of Philos. Was there hope for them? "May it be so."

"Tell me, Agios," the priest asked softly, "can you read?"

Agios smiled. "Oh, yes, I can read very well. Several languages, in fact."

"The scrolls that Nicholas's father left for him—you have them?"

In answer, Agios put the pouch on the table.

"Nicholas may have told you of these. They are the Gospels, the good news of Jesus and His mission," he said in almost a whisper.

"He read his favorite passages aloud to me," Agios said.

"They make up the most important scriptures of our faith. They were first written down by Jesus's disciples and copied and recopied by faithful scribes in the generations since. Can you prove to me that you can read them?"

Agios took one of the scrolls at random and partly unrolled it. He read aloud: *"In the beginning was the Word . . ."* When Eudemus didn't interrupt, Agios read on for a few sentences, ending with the words *". . . and the light shines in darkness, and the darkness has not understood it."*

Then the priest said, "That's enough. I see you can read. That's the Gospel of John."

"Strange words," Agios said. "I'm like the darkness—I can't understand them."

"You will when you've read more. Agios, don't stop at Nicholas's favorite parts. Instead, read completely though these. They'll answer your questions better than I could." He rose. "It's late, and I must return home. Thank you, Agios, for taking care of the boy."

"No. Thank you."

The priest left him there. For much of the night he sat at the table, bathed in the yellow lamplight, reading and rereading the scrolls, absorbing a story he already knew by heart.

Chapter 19

Morning came, and with it Nicholas, bringing bread warm from the hearth with honey, dates, and milk, and the boy placed it carefully on the center of the table in his father's study where Agios had been sitting for hours. He didn't say anything, but stood with his hands clasped in front of him, waiting for Agios to greet him.

Of course, Agios was aware of the boy, but he was retracing the narrative of a passage he had grown to love. *He is not here. He is risen just as he said . . .*

He absentmindedly stroked the scar along his cheek, the sign of his great failure.

If he rose—perhaps I did not fail. Perhaps.

When he looked up, Nicholas still stood there, a small frown creasing his mouth.

"Good morning, friend," Agios said, carefully rolling up the scroll. "I owe you an apology. We traveled too hard yesterday. I trust you had a good rest?"

Nicholas exhaled impatiently. "I'm fine, Agios. I don't need an apology from you."

Agios couldn't help teasing him a bit. "Then what *do* you need, Nicholas?"

The boy would have stamped his foot if he were younger, but he settled for balling his fist and hitting it against his own thigh. "I want to *know*, Agios. The answer to the question I asked you in your cave: Do you believe?"

Agios didn't know whether to laugh or cry. It was still a question he couldn't answer, even after the hours he had spent reading the scrolls, reliving the stories that they contained. He wasn't mentioned, of course, but he could picture himself on the periphery, observing so much of it but understanding so little. How many of the people who had known Jesus could truly say that they understood who he was and what he intended to do?

"I don't know," Agios said after a long minute had passed.

But the shadow of a sad smile crossed his face. "I don't truly know what it means to believe in something. In someone."

"It means that we are sure of what we hope for and certain of what we do not see." Nicholas pulled up a chair across from Agios and sat forward with his elbows on the table. He was so trusting, so earnest. It was obvious how much he wanted Agios to have faith.

"Those are lovely words," Agios said.

"They're from Hebrews." Then, sensing Agios's confusion, he gestured at the scrolls scattered over the table in his father's study. "It's one of these, but I couldn't tell you which one."

Agios sighed. "I don't think I'm up to reading more scrolls right now anyway. I don't know what I'm supposed to do at all, Nicholas." He bowed his head and murmured, "I've worked so hard to deserve the mercy of Christ and his forgiveness—and yet, it never comes."

"But it has come, Agios. You don't have to *do* anything."

"But—"

"That's God's glory," Nicholas interrupted excitedly. "Grace is something we're given, not something we earn or take. All we have to do is accept what's been done for us. Jesus died for me, Agios. And he died for you, too."

For me. After all I've done. And all I couldn't do.

I am undeserving.

Agios felt as if his heart were a bottomless pit, black and carved into ground that had been poisoned by years of grief and brutality and death. He had killed people. He had watched others die. He had wished for his own death and tried to make it happen more than once.

"I'm not sure I understand," Agios finally whispered.

At this, Nicholas sat up straight and smiled at him. "Oh, you'll never understand. Nobody expects you to understand the mind of God or know why he would love us in the midst of our weakness and sin. I think . . ." He paused, considering. "I think this is a matter for the heart. Do you love him?"

The answer was on Agios's lips before he had a chance to wonder if it was true or not.

Love him? That's why I followed him when he was a baby and why I prayed to follow him until his mission was complete. That's why I felt so changed when I sat near the Sychar well. That's why my heart broke when I saw him die on the cross.

Whenever he and Krampus had caught a glimpse of Jesus, Agios had felt his spirit soar.

"I do," he said, his conviction unswerving.

"Agios, you were forgiven long ago. God has accepted your repentance. He gives his forgiveness freely."

Agios smiled back. But it was hard to accept that anything could be that simple.

"You'll see," Nicholas assured him, his eyes sparkling.

When he was alone, Agios wondered, *Should I just leave now? Nicholas needs a father, and I—I need a son. But how can I be a father to him when all my sons die?* And how could he tell Nicholas the truth about himself—that he was a cursed man who could not die?

I couldn't save Philos, or Krampus—or Jesus! I swore to protect him, and I couldn't save him! How can I tell Nicholas of my curse?

With despair, Agios bowed his head. "I think I believe," he murmured. "Help me to believe! Let me know—did you make others like me? If you did—are we blessed or cursed? Help me understand."

No answer came, and Agios could only hope that, somehow, from somewhere, one would come.

Father Eudemus came again that morning, and Agios thanked him. The priest said, "I think you've been good for Nicholas."

"The other way around," Agios said. "He's been good for me."

Nona laughed at this, throwing back her head in delight. "That boy influences everyone he meets!" she cried. "I bet he hasn't told you."

"Told me what?"

"Nona, please," the younger Nicholas warned, giving his caretakers a look of distress.

"It's nothing to be ashamed of," the priest told him. Then he turned to Agios. "Our Nicholas said to me he wants to distribute every coin of his inheritance among the poor. He quoted the scripture to me."

Nona said, "'If you want to be perfect, go, sell your possessions and give to the poor, and you will have treasure in heaven. Then come, follow me.' That's what Jesus said."

Agios recognized the passage. He had read it more than once during his long night. "Matthew?" he guessed.

Nicholas shrugged. "Or Mark or Luke. The story is recorded in all three, but the message is always the same: Jesus knew how easily our hearts were corrupted."

"So many in town are needy after the plague," the priest said. "It's a wonderful gift, Nicholas."

"I'm going to be a priest anyway," Nicholas mumbled, clearly embarrassed. "What need do I have for money?"

But there was no diminishing what Nicholas had done. Agios felt his heart swell with pride as if the boy were his own son. He had squandered his life searching and hungering, killing and carving a way for himself in the world. Even at such a young age, Nicholas lived another way. What was the difference?

Jesus.

Agios felt his voice waver as he said, "I told you not so long ago that you will be a fine man, Nicholas. I think I was wrong. I think you already are a fine man."

The priest and Nona promised to care for Nicholas— "I won't let him become entirely poor until he joins the priesthood," Eudemus assured Agios with a twinkle.

Agios bade them farewell. Without the boy, the trip back to the cave was rapid, but all the same, Agios was surprised when he reached the meadow where Nicholas grazed his flock every spring well before sundown. He climbed the slope quickly, hurrying although nothing awaited his care. Surely weeds hadn't sprung up to overtake the garden in one night. And he had nothing worth stealing.

As he often did when troubled or worried, Agios stepped into his little storage room and selected some good oak, the pure white heartwood shading into a thick layer of fine-grained tan. His carving tools were in a relatively new goatskin satchel and he slung the strap over his shoulder, wondering for the first time at his need for a new pouch, but not new blades.

Crouching near his fire pit, Agios unrolled the kit and looked at the small precise instruments. When had he last sharpened them? He could no longer remember. They should have dulled with use, or they should have rusted to pieces. Agios had ceased to count the years, but in Nicholas's home he had learned the date. It had been almost three hundred years since Gamos had made a gift of these exact tools for him. Three hundred years.

And yet they kept their edge, always ready to do their work, seemingly immune to age and blunting and rust. It sent a little chill down his spine.

What had he prayed? All those . . . centuries ago?

Let me serve him until his mission is completed.

Agios began to carve, not consciously planning on the result, but letting his hands do the work automatically.

We have only one life. We may waste it, or we may use it to learn of God and what God wants for us. And we all make mistakes. Only one life.

Except for me. I've been cursed—

No. Blessed. I've been blessed with many lifetimes—and I've wasted too many in regrets and blame and guilt.

As he carved, he prayed: "Forgive me for not knowing you were with me the whole time—Krampus understood that. I should have known when I first saw the infant Jesus, or when I heard his words at the well."

He began to shake and with a broken voice added, "I should have known at the cross! Forgive my stubbornness. Give me the water of life. I will drink!"

The sky was darkening to purple when he realized that the figure taking shape beneath his agile fingers was Jesus. But this time, he wasn't a baby. He was grown, God and man, triumphant in robes of white and holding high—in blessing, in welcome—his beautiful, nail-scarred hands.

And Agios wept.

Chapter 20

S ometimes, transformation is quick. A rock dropped in a quiet pool disturbs the surface into ripples. An unexpected thunderstorm blows up out of nowhere in the middle of a sunny summer day.

Sometimes, though, transformation comes slowly. It's the air warming a little every day, pools of water forming on the surface of an icebound lake. Then drops cascade from trees, creating rivulets on cracking ground that become streams and rivers and rushing waterfalls. Brown grasses turn green by degrees, brightening as the sun warms the earth and coaxes buds to emerge from branches and turn their plump faces to the sun. The world becomes utterly different, wholly unrecognizable from the place it once was, and yet the process is always a surprise. To the sleeping heart, one day it is winter. And the next, spring.

But it's never that straightforward.

How long does it take for us to truly understand? How can we look right past a simple truth that is plain to any child?

Agios would continue to find his role. His metamorphosis would stretch over centuries, though its essentials were already set: He had a father's loving heart and a strong man's tender hands. The hard years had taught him perseverance, and he had always been generous. Others had seen it—Philos, certainly, and Gamos, Caspar, the others . . . Krampus. In the end, the last person to accept the truth about him was himself.

Nicholas took up his studies in Myra, a town not too far from his birthplace of Patara. And because Agios was ready for a life beyond the isolation he had known for so long, because he knew that he was teetering on the edge of something so much greater than himself—belief!—he visited his young friend often.

Several times a year, Agios left his cave and made the journey to Myra—a trek insignificant for a man of his stature and energy—and learned at the feet of his young friend, his new son. Agios couldn't get enough of the stories and teachings of the man he so openly loved, for even the name *Jesus* was enough to bring a smile to his craggy face.

"More," he would plead with Nicholas. "Tell me more."

And the boy, who had grown into a man, obliged.

Nicholas had other lessons to teach. When he became a priest, he felt keenly the need of the poor people of Myra, those the Romans spurned. Agios learned that Nicholas worked hard to learn of poor people who deserved help—and to give it to them. However, he gave secretly, never revealing himself. "Why?" Agios asked him once.

"Well," Nicholas said seriously, "I think that all good gifts come ultimately from God. It wouldn't do for the messenger to take credit for his master's work."

He recalled a mountain, and a distant figure in white preaching to a multitude. *Give your gifts secretly and don't seek glory from them. God, who sees all secrets, knows what you have done and will reward you.*

Oh, Agios remembered. All that became real one cool night. Agios had come in late on one of his trips to the city, and Nicholas, expecting him, had waited for hours to meet him near the gates. Then as Agios and Nicholas walked the streets of Myra, deep in conversation, they turned a corner and Agios felt Nicholas grip his arm above the elbow. "Look there," Nicholas said quietly.

Ahead of them in an empty lot, three people clustered around a small fire. They were poorly dressed—a man, a woman, and a little girl of six or seven. They leaned toward the warmth and the light of the humble fire they had built in an out-of-the way spot, a walled garden that had become overgrown with weeds.

Something came over Agios the moment he saw them. *All good gifts come from God.*

A voice, or just in his head?

Agios reached into his pack and brought out a doll, one that he had cleverly fitted with joints so its limbs and head could move. Its eyes even opened and closed. He held it up so that Nicholas could see, and his friend smiled and nodded.

Agios jerked his head, and he and Nicholas backed around the corner again. He knelt and placed the doll on the pavement, just where the girl might see it. As he began to rise, suddenly Nicholas bent and placed a little jingling bag of coins next to the doll. "They will need food and shelter as well," Nicholas said softly.

Agios stepped out. He wore the same red garment that Nicholas had given him years ago. He stood until the girl glanced up and saw him, and then he beckoned, pointed down, and then walked away, Nicholas falling into step beside him. "You wish no credit for your art?" Nicholas asked.

"The only one who should know about it does know," Agios replied. Behind them, he heard the man cry out in astonished delight. He felt warm and did not look back.

"That was kind of you," Nicholas said.

"Son, you taught me that giving is a way of serving God," Agios said. "I'd like to help you in your works of charity, if you'll let me."

That moment changed everything for Agios. The next time he traveled to Myra he crammed as many trinkets as he could into his sack, along with dried goat's meat, a bag of coins—the last remnants of the scholar-kings' reward to him—a warm cloak he had traded for, as well as a sack of oranges that he had harvested from a grove a half day's journey away.

He told Nicholas, "I was wrong to think I could earn redemption."

Nicholas, now a middle-aged man and an honored priest, murmured, "No one can do that, father. God's forgiveness is a gift." He added warmly, "You of all men should surely understand the nature of a gift!"

Agios sighed. "All those years I lived without hope, with guilt and bitterness boiling in my heart. I never paused to think of all the others who were even worse off. I could have helped so many times and didn't."

"Hope," Nicholas murmured. "That is the greatest gift you offer others."

Distributing the goods was a delight. Just as in the days when Agios left his carvings for children to find, he had the distinct pleasure of giving gifts without his recipient knowing the origin. A woman toiled over a pot of lentils and broth until Agios slipped past and there was suddenly—miraculously almost—mutton on her table. A young scholar walked home from classes, his head heavy and shoulders hunched until a perfect orange appeared on the ground before his shuffling feet.

"They're talking about you, you know," Nicholas told him once.

More years had passed, thought it felt like a mere season to Agios. A bearded Nicholas wore the robes of a bishop—red, like the coat that Nicholas had given Agios on the mountain, but a rich brocade, long and tasseled and trimmed in gold and white.

Nicholas's robes weren't the only thing that had changed in the decades since Agios had first met him. Eudemus had been right: the emperor Diocletian had turned against the Christians with violence and the force of Roman law. In parts of the Roman Empire churches were razed, scriptures burned, Christians tormented and executed.

"What do you mean, they're talking about me?" Agios was going through his bag, taking inventory of what he had given and what remained to be distributed.

"Your gifts," Nicholas said, as if they should be past the point of pretending. "They say you're a miracle, a saint, the hand of God himself. Some say you're my uncle Nicholas, who was known for charity, come back to help the poor."

"I don't know anything about that."

His old friend laughed. "A red coat," he teased. "They always see a flash of red after a blessing appears."

"Nonsense."

Nicholas said suddenly, "Other people think that it's me."

Agios studied Nicholas's red robe, the way his long beard had grown gray in the years since they had first met. When had his friend aged so? It sobered him to think that so much time had passed, and yet, he could see how the man he considered a son could almost be mistaken for him. "Does this bother you?" Agios asked.

"I want no glory," Nicholas said sincerely. "Let those who want to give thanks for bounty thank Jesus himself, the fount of all blessings."

"You are his hands and feet," Agios said. "And my generosity springs from your well, my son. You inspire me."

For just a moment, Nicholas grinned like a child. It flashed across his face so bright and sweet that Agios felt his heart catch in his chest. "We are twins, you and I," he said with a glint in his eye. "I know your secrets, Nicholas. I know about the dowries!"

Nicholas laughed.

"The story is on everyone's lips. You threw three bags of gold through the window of a poor man's house so his daughters wouldn't be sold into slavery!"

"The earth is the Lord's and everything in it," Nicholas said with a shrug. "What is gold to me?"

Now Agios was laughing. "They say it landed in stockings left before the fire to dry."

"My aim isn't that good. Tales grow in the telling!"

After a moment, Agios added, "Tale or not, you've started a tradition, you know. I hear children are hanging their stockings over the hearth in the hope that you may visit their house one night."

"Then we shall make sure they are not disappointed," Nicholas said.

They worked together whenever they could, distributing bread where bellies were empty and shoes where feet went bare.

Nicholas's reputation grew, and it wasn't long before Agios himself felt humbled by the stories he heard. A boy, snatched into slavery and missing for months, appeared healthy and whole in his parents' home, still clutching the golden cup he had carried for some faraway king. A storm was calmed, an innocent set free, there was food in the midst of famine. And through it all, Nicholas and Agios spread the name of the one who gave it all so that every tongue sang his praises: *Jesus, Jesus, Jesus.*

When the Romans imprisoned Nicholas, no one was

much surprised. But though Agios's heart ached, he couldn't abandon the vision that he and Nicholas had so earnestly embraced. Agios redoubled his efforts. The man in the red coat was everywhere and nowhere: extending compassion, inspiring peace, spreading hope.

One night, as Agios left a basket on the doorstep of a widow's modest home, the door opened. Agios froze, waiting for her to shriek in alarm at this stranger standing on her doorstep. Instead, a smile broke across her face and she threw the door open to take his huge, rough hands in her own small, soft ones.

"Is it you?" she whispered in awe. "Bishop Nicholas, is it you?"

Agios ducked his head. "No. Just a friend," he murmured.

"Thank you!" she said. "Oh, thank you. I didn't know if—I thought that with Bishop Nicholas in jail we had no hope."

Tears shimmered on her cheeks in the pale moonlight, and Agios was overcome with compassion for her. "We are Christ's ambassadors," he told her. "Bishop Nicholas and I, but you, too, my daughter. We are *all* his hands and feet."

She squeezed his hands and whispered a prayer of

thanksgiving. And as Agios left, he glanced over his shoulder and saw that despite her own need, instead of carrying the entire basket into her own tiny house, she first took a loaf of bread and laid it at her neighbor's door.

Surely, it was the start of something beautiful.

Emperors fell and rose. Constantine, more tolerant than Diocletian, and finally a Christian himself, took the throne. Nicholas was released from prison and given more honor than ever. Agios found his old friend thin and scarred, his face drawn and tired, but his eyes were still warm and bright.

"What have they done to you?" Agios cried.

"It doesn't matter," Nicholas said putting his hand on his old friend's shoulder. "Scripture tells us everyone who wants to live a godly life in Christ Jesus will be persecuted. 'We glory in our sufferings because we know that suffering produces perseverance, perseverance character, and character, hope.'"

Agios finished, "'And hope does not put us to shame, because God's love has been poured out into our hearts.'" He searched Nicholas's face. It was open and inviting, the sort of countenance that made you want to linger and listen.

"Love is never safe," Nicholas said. "It is always a danger, a great and beautiful risk. But I take it gladly, Father."

Father. Even now the word gave Agios a twinge of regret for the past—though he did love Nicholas as a son.

Agios reached out and clasped Nicholas's hand, drawing it to his chest where he could hold it tight against his heart. "And so do I, my son." It was a covenant between them, a promise that all that had happened, everything that had come before, would pale in the glory of all that was to come.

It was just the beginning.

Chapter 21

S ometimes death is a simple thing.

Nicholas's death was not.

He was seventy-five years old and a bishop when his body began to fail. One day he struggled to read his scrolls and the next he listed to the side when he walked. It pained Agios to watch his friend deteriorate by degrees, but Nicholas accepted everything cheerfully.

"I am an old man!" he told Agios. "And I have nothing to fear. My life is safe in Christ."

"I know, son," Agios said. He carefully rolled up the scroll they had been studying and rose to put it away. Death was a topic he could hardly bear to discuss. It made him think of the ones he had lost—and reminded him that he would soon add another loved one to the growing list. It filled him with an emotion that he was neither comfortable with nor proud of: envy. When would it be his turn? When would he close his eyes and open them in the presence of Jesus? And Krampus? And Philos? His soul yearned for this above all things.

One last secret remained between him and Nicholas, one truth that stood like a wall separating them. But why was he hiding? Nicholas was his dearest friend, his teacher and advisor. His *son*.

"Nicholas," Agios said, rejoining him at the table. "I must tell you something."

Nicholas's eyes had drifted shut, but he opened them now and fixed Agios with a slow smile. "You have my attention."

"Have you—" Agios wasn't sure how to begin. "Have you noticed anything different about me? I mean, compared to other men."

His laugh was still a joyful sound, though Nicholas wheezed. "Father, everything is different about you." But the serious look on Agios's face seemed to make him rethink his answer. Gently, he said, "You are set apart, Agios.

I don't know how or why, but you are not like other men. You are fast and strong, tireless. You haven't aged a day since I met you when I was just a boy, yet I am now old and about to go home."

Agios was surprised. "Why didn't you say anything?"

"I trust you, my father. I knew you would tell me in good time. And if you didn't, I thought it wasn't a secret for me to know. I asked you about it once, remember?"

Agios did remember. Nicholas had still been a child then. One night as they sat together he had studied Agios's hands and asked, "How old are you, Agios?"

There was no answer for that. Besides he didn't want to scare the boy. "As old as my tongue and a little older than my teeth." He paused and smiled. "I'll tell you when you have a white beard of your own," he said.

Nicholas hadn't pressed him further.

"Agios," Nicholas said gently, "my beard is now as white as yours."

"I was there," Agios said in a rush, knowing that Nicholas would believe him, that he could finally unburden himself of his own bewildering story. "I saw Jesus." He touched his left cheek. "I got this scar when the Romans crucified him."

The tale came out over the course of days and Nicholas faded bit by bit. By the time they reached the heart-break of Jesus's crucifixion, Nicholas lay confined to his bed. Still, he would murmur his delight at certain parts of Agios's account. And sometimes, Agios would use a cloth to wipe the tears that collected in his old friend's eyes.

"Such a gift," Nicholas whispered. Agios had thought his friend was sleeping. His eyes were closed, his breath too shallow, too quick.

"I've always thought it was a curse," Agios said.

Nicholas's eyes flashed open. "God gives good gifts to his children," he insisted. "We are all a part of the body; we each have a role to fulfill. Yours is remarkable."

"I never understood," Agios confessed.

Tenderly, the old bishop said, "Oh, Agios, I told you long ago. You are worthy, and God forgave you before you ever thought you needed it. You asked humbly and with a broken spirit and God heard your prayer and transformed you into a different man."

"Humble?" Agios asked, shaking his head. "Me?"

Nicholas took his hand. "You're the most humble person I know. The scars on your hands and your face were earned by serving others. Don't you feel that your scarred heart was made whole the moment you gave your service to Christ?"

"My son," Agios said, clasping the aged hand. "I didn't know! Not until you taught me—even when you were only a child, you showed me what it means to give without grudging, to live with love. Nicholas, I *saw* Jesus, but I never *knew* him—not until you showed me the way. How long does it take for a man like me to understand? Help me again. I once prayed that God would allow me to serve him until Jesus's mission was through, but I don't know how to do that."

Nicholas squeezed Agios's hand with his frail fingers. "You need no help, my friend. How can any of us understand it all, the gift from that baby you guarded, from that holy man who died on the cross? It doesn't ask understanding, but only acceptance. Your prayer has been answered. You've become a legend, a guardian, and a mystery."

"What do you mean?" Agios gripped Nicholas's hand even tighter, but just like that, Nicholas had fallen asleep.

The others Agios had mourned had died by violence, or suddenly, and this slow decline was one of the most heartbreaking things he had ever encountered. Nicholas drifted in and out of consciousness, and sometimes when he opened his eyes Agios could see recognition there. Other times it was as if Nicholas was already gone.

For two days Agios didn't leave his beloved son's side. Then, late one night, Nicholas took a deep breath and whispered his first words in days. They were clear and lovely, a call to arms: "Persevere, Agios. Until Jesus's mission is complete. Until all the ends of the earth shall hear. Remind all mankind to fight the good fight. Remind them to give in memory of God's greatest gift. Give them comfort and hope. Promise me, Father."

Agios swallowed. "I promise—Father."

Nicholas's smile was gentle. "You've never called me that before."

"You are a priest," Agios said simply.

Nicholas drew a deep breath. Then his features relaxed, and his smile became a look of expectancy—of delight.

He didn't breathe again.

Tears dripped off Agios's cheeks as he leaned over his friend. He kissed his forehead in blessing, in good-bye. "Farewell, Son. Farewell—Father."

His back bent with the burden of loss—"But God gave me a back for bearing burdens," he whispered to himself. He stood beside the bed.

The whole town mourned Nicholas's passing. With his own hands Agios carried the frail body to the tomb and placed it safely inside. *I have buried three sons now*, he thought.

But now he hoped to see them all again, in the fullness of time.

The priests of the church thought of Agios as a faithful servant of the bishop's. They offered him a place among them, but he gently refused. One asked, "What do you want, then? You deserve something."

"There is one thing," he said. They were surprised when he named it, for it was only a well-worn garment that Nicholas had set aside years before, but they gladly gave it to him.

"Is that all?" the priest asked gently.

Agios said, "Father Nicholas gave me a gift already. This is plenty."

Hesitantly, the priest asked, "Sir, some say you are the bishop's uncle—Nicholas, too. Is that your name?"

"It's a good name," Agios said. *Yes. I would be honored to share it.*

Despite the offers of hospitality, Nicholas took the red cloak back to his small room and sat looking at it. It was a symbol of the true, precious gift that Nicholas had left him, one so priceless it took his breath away. Already he could feel himself fading into mist and memory, a myth of a man who would point to the cross and beyond—to the resurrection. His role was to teach men and women how to give—and to give them all what Agios himself had always needed:

Hope.

Agios would remind them all of Christ and his promise, and he would inspire them to follow his example, to serve until Jesus's mission was truly complete, until all the ends of the earth would hear and believe.

Agios took Nicholas's cloak and swept it over his own shoulders. It was a perfect fit. The robe spilled to the floor in lustrous folds, and the gold and white hems sparkled in the lamplight. Agios turned up the hood, hiding his face save his long, snowy beard, shouldered his pack, and left the room.

The night was cold and clear, the stars a million points of light in the dark veil above him. But one star glowed especially for him. The North Star that had graced the sky when he was still a boy so many years ago shone eternally in the heavens, winking as if God Himself were whispering to Agios.

Maybe He was.

Glory.

Glory and majesty, honor and praise, all glory to the highest.

Agios knew he had become a part of the story that would transform the world. It had the power to make men and women whole, to change everything, because it had already changed everything in him.

Until all the ends of the earth shall hear.

"Lead me home," Agios whispered, a prayer that would live on his lips in the days and years and ages to come. And then he shouldered his pack and started walking north, toward that place where the stars always shone clearest.

Though he walked through darkness, his heart was filled with light, for he knew that his work was only just beginning. The entirety of his life to this point had merely been to prepare him for what he was to do next: bring hope to the hopeless and joy to the joyless. He would serve mankind by reminding them every year that a King had been born who had died for their sins.

There, at the top of the world, Agios would spend long nights watching the frigid sky, waiting for the one star that would never set. That impossibly bright star, which had first appeared at a time of great sadness and anger in his life, would usher in a new era of joy and celebration.

For when that star returned to the heavens, the Lord would return from the heavens to the earth.